I0651641

Alice Kingsbury

Secrets told

With twenty-two piquant illustrations from life

Alice Kingsbury

Secrets told
With twenty-two piquant illustrations from life

ISBN/EAN: 9783743303263

Manufactured in Europe, USA, Canada, Australia, Japa

Cover: Foto ©Andreas Hilbeck / pixelio.de

Manufactured and distributed by brebook publishing software
(www.brebook.com)

Alice Kingsbury

Secrets told

SECRETS TOLD.

With Twenty-two Piquant Illustrations

From Life.

BY

ALICE KINGSBURY

(MRS. COL. F. M. COOLEY)

SAN FRANCISCO :

ALTA CALIFORNIA PRINTING HOUSE 529 CALIFORNIA STREET

1879

CONTENTS.

*First published in the Argonaut.
†First published in the Chronicle.
‡An unknown writer in the Chronicle.
§First published in the Chronicle.

SECRETS TOLD.

I am a bachelor of—to observers—an uncertain age. My lady friends make me their confidant. I don't know why, unless it is my sympathetic, reassuring ways. We all know that some people invite confidence without an effort on their part, as other people repel the same. I am of the former. Now mind me, in giving these conversations to the public, I betray no trust reposed in me, for I so change the names and locations, that the people cannot be recognized by their nearest neighbors. I do it too, to help the dear sex with which I so sympathize, in their troubles, disappointments, and the thousand and one petty annoyances of married life. I do it to help them correct any faults of their own that have in any possible way contributed to their unhappiness. I do it that they may quietly drop the book in their husbands' way, so that they can see the trouble, the little faults of Jones or Smith cause to their wives and families, and so be tempted to mentally examine themselves.

I wish and expect my book to do good, am almost certain some of the sketches already have, for which I thus publicly thank the *Alta*, who first lent me a helping hand in the hard and difficult path of literature.

Some may object that I have spoken too plainly—that the good old Saxon words have not been dressed enough for polite society. In reply, I will say, the book is for grown people; it is intended to correct abuses, which only plain, truthful language can; milk and water words would do no good, and as all that I have written has really happened, with, as I said before, a little alteration, I would beg those whom the book offends to give it where it will do the most good —or put it in the fire.   Hop o-My-Thumb.

P. S.—It was the intention of the writer to receive lady subscribers only, but finding, although it was very sure it was rather too slow for his purpose—for the reason for the aforesaid slowness, see book—he therefore announces that the subscription list is open to the masculine gender also.

Secrets Told.

BUTTONS OFF.

N. B.—This being woman's first duty, thus I begin my book.

"Oh! good gracious! Oh, my! ho! ho! ha!"

"What is the matter, Pet?"

"Oh, dear! to think! the very first one! ho! ho! ho!"

"Why, Pet, you'll go into a fit, if you don't stop."

"Ho! ho! ho!—ho! ho! ho!"

His face was red and swollen, and the little woman became alarmed, so taking him by the two hands, she tried to raise him from the bed, where he had thrown himself in the excess of his hilarity. It was hard work, for his two hundred avoirdupois was too much for her ligh' weight of eighty-five. After a few more outbursts of "Ho! ho! ho!' and the sprinkling of his face with cold water—sprinkling, mind you, by a gentle, loving hand—not dashed on by a vixen—he helped him. self to a sitting position on the edge of the bed.

"Pet, you frighten me!"

"But to think, the very first—ho! ho!—"

"Now, please, don't!"

And all this about a button being off!! She had told him, with a great deal of pride: "Pet, I have mended all your shirts, and there's not a button off now, in the whole lot."

The Shirt.

"Let's see," he had replied, incredulously; and sure enough, the very first shirt was minus a button. She tried to explain it away, but the fact was indisputable. She wasn't a very good housekeeper, and sometimes forgot to attend to those very important—to women—articles of buttons, while she was, well, not exactly attending to the wants of Borrioboola Gha, but writing poetry. (This is a true story, as the fairy books don't say.)

They were a happy couple, too; it was only when clean shirt day came round, and the drawer was suddenly opened, that her face became anxious, and she tried to remember if she had forgotten to look at the wash last week, and often her fears were confirmed by

"Humph! there's a —— button off!"

"Is there, really? Why, I looked—"

"No you didn't, either! I shouldn't think it was much work to sew on a button!"

"But, Pet, if you only knew how hard it was to put a shirt away decently, after completely unfolding it to look at every cuff and neck-band, you would not be surprised that I content myself, sometimes, by seeing that the bosoms are all right—here, let me sew one on." So she sits up in her nightgown, her teeth chattering with cold, and he bends over, looking the picture of amiability. "The more haste the less speed," you know the adage; and whoever saw a button sewed on in a hurry that the thread didn't knot several times, or the button fall to the floor, or the needle stick somebody, so that there are generally two sighs of relief when the operation is completed?

The quickest process I ever saw yet of arousing a slumbering woman on a cold morning, has been the gentle exclamation of her spouse:

"There's a button off."

It is said so quietly, too, without any dashes, as we gentlemen always remind our wives of their little deficiencies in duty, that it is a marvel how it can have the effect of a thunderbolt, causing an apparition in white to start up with such suddenness as to nearly knock her nightcap off her head, more potent than the aroma of a good breakfast stealing up-stairs, or the sweet tones of love, uttering :

"Get up, dear."

Now, let us look at this question theoretically.

A button is a small thing, a cheap thing, a thing of little intrinsic value ; a piece of pearl, a piece of china or a piece of brass, or bone, or iron, or tin, or silk, or cloth, with one hole, two holes, three, four, and sometimes no hole at all, still, a button's a button and very dear to the heart of a man.

Pins answer every purpose for you, gentle women ; your deft fingers can pin a collar or a ruff on your dress, and the pins remain as firm as adamant, and don't draw blood either ; but let one of us poor mascu- lines try it in a fit of spleen or resentment, and don't we rue the day ? Why, there's not a man on the street that don't know it ; either by seeing the pin, that we have not the ingenuity to conceal, and that constantly rasps our hands as we stroke our petted moustache, or by the collar getting into our back hair, leaving a rosy line of flesh where the pin has been making its mark, or by that peculiar twisting and turning of the neck that cannot be mistaken.

Now, we don't mind our cuffs being a little "sawy" at the edges, for, although I was a little surprised at my friend ——l stretching out his from a sleeve of finest broadcloth, to pencil a memoranda of how much he was "long" or "short" on New Coso, although I was, as I said, surprised to see a nice little saw at the end of his snow-white cuff still I know if the buttons were all on, he was in comfort and could smile at the ragged edge.

I have heard of a murder being committed because a beefsteak was not done to suit ; of another, because dinner was not done in time;

of scores of others on more frivolous pretexts; yet who ever heard of blood being drawn by patient man on account of an aggravation fifty, nay a hundred times worse than either of these? But, dear ladies, take warning, the mildest of men can be driven to desperation ; the most amiable of husbands can become a fiend ; the most learned of scholars turn brute ; the most loving of spouses a savage, by the constant, reiterated, inexcusable, with malice-aforethought forgetfulness of the first and foremost duty of a married woman's life, attending to her husband's buttons.

Ladies, be warned! Farewell.

And this was Madeline's experience, related to me.

Hop-O'-My-Thumb.

SCOLDING.

We don't scold. With all our faults of omission and commission, we don't scold. Why, everybody knows that, from our wife down to our youngest babe. That is the fair sex's prerogative. If we refuse them the ballot, for goodness sake, let us grant them the privilege of expressing their mind freely.

Of course, we would rather they would express in words than in actions, for it is a little unpleasant to have to go about for a day or two with our face bound up, because of a dreadful boil, when it's only the loving marks of little nails, we are trying to hide.

A friend of mine, living in the cold North—a politician, too—had occasion once to come into town—he resided in the country. He met several of his colleagues, and, as politicians never drink anything strong, he was surprised that after imbibing several glasses of milk, and smoking sundry cigars, that he should wake up as a visitor in the jail, not as a prisoner, mind you, for he was a noted politician and the jailor, his friend, took this method of hiding him from the gaze of the rude public. When he did not return to his home at the proper time —some men have proper times, and some don't, as we know—his wife, who adored the ground he walked on, figuratively speaking, had had an immense feather-bed placed in their large wagon ; then, with the driver, started for town in the middle of the night, expecting to pick up his poor, mangled body on the road. The twelve miles were passed, and no mangled body; the town was reached, and no rumor of such a body. The patient wife visited all his haunts, and finally brought up at the jail. Her entrance suddenly awakened her husband, who quickly remembered he had forgotten several hours, and could not imagine how in the world he had got there! She quietly took him to a friend's to explain matters. He smiled so good-naturedly, by way of explanation, that it exasperated her, and she clawed his face like an infuriated little cat. All for love, though! Why, for her, the sun rose and set in that man's beautiful black whiskers.

Think how she had suffered!—a twelve-mile ride in a bitter cold night, straining her eyes at every log and shadow; and not to find his man-gled body after all!—her kindness thrown away on an ungrateful man who had only been—well, indiscreet. He carried the marks of those lov-ing fingers for several days, but he didn't scold —at least, I did not hear him. I don't know what he did when he reached home.

This is the Face.

Now, this is a sample of what we poor men endure without a mur-mer—sometimes; and for such little offences, too!

Why, I know of a man who tried to pursuade his wife that she must have his dinner done in time, by quietly pressing his feet on her body! The argument was not effective, though, for she never cooked his dinner again, and he was not hung for murder, either. This happened in the enlightened town of Cincinnati.

But men will express their minds by actions, leaving words to women, in other cities beside that. Why, last Summer in gentle Philadelphia, that mis-named City of Brotherly Love, a man used the peaceful argument of saturating his wife with coal oil, and then igniting her, all about a beefsteak! You will find the account in the left hand column of one of the daily papers there; she died, and the man lives, for all I know.

Now, though we dont scold, I would advise the abandonment of these very pronounced arguments, as the result is neither satisfactory, nor the record of the experience calculated to help a needy brother.

We don't like scolds of any kind, and to be eternally greeted with: "Now, Hun"—short for Honey—"do be careful, and wipe your feet!"—meaning boots. "Oh, dear! see how you have soiled the carpet! !"

"Can't you possibly spit straighter into that cuspador?"

" Please don't smoke in the parlor, it spoils the curtains?"

" Oh, dear!—with a weary sigh—" you've got your boots on the bed again!"

Are apt to irritate a man, and cause him to leave his peaceful home and seek elsewhere an asylum in which he can indulge his little eccentricities.

The corner grocery is very convenient, though it is a little unpleasant to be startled from a quiet game of whist, or lively draw-poker, by the dulcet tones of your wife, who makes a loaf of bread, or to know the exact time, an excuse for a visit; and seeing our elbows extending beyond the inconveniently small barricade that separates our elysium from the gaze of impertinent curiosity, she instantly recognizes that patch on our sleeve, and exclaims: "why Major! Some one has been waiting a whole hour for you!"

We jump up lively, thinking it's that Jones who has been owing us for so long, come to settle ; but are soon undeceived when we reach the gate, or perhaps she is shrewd and lets us reach the parlor first.

"Now, aren't you a pretty husband! Here I'm moping all day alone, and the minute you get your dinner," etc., etc.—*we have all been there.*

Now ladies, don't, please don't scold?

I would rather my wife would slap my ears good, so long as she did not scratch my face, than to be forever nag, nag, naging at me.

Two of our friends went to a country ball one night, leaving their wives in ignorance at the hotel. There they watched for them till the gray dawn, when they returned—one looking very crestfallen, the other jolly, with a horsewhip in his hand.

"Here love, use this on me, but don't scold!" said he; so she was silenced before she began.

"Whew" whispered the other, "I wouldn't dare offer it to my wife; she'd—she'd cut my very heart out!'"

Now, here was a small offence to be even angry at. A gentleman enjoys himself, dancing till day with a lot of pretty girls, and his wife, who should be so thankful that he was happy, and who should look upon her long night of dreadful anxiety as a mere bagatelle to be often endured, if necessary, to allow him the ecstasy of squeezing slender waists and pressing soft hands, to be angry! Now, what reasonable woman ought to object, and to scold, too. Oh! dreadful!

Now, if our wives should follow our example, and do likewise, we would not scold. Oh, no! But we would *kill!* or send them home to their mothers. That's more polite and genteel.

I once knew a man who scolded sometimes, but he was the mildest

tempered man in the world; so fat and jolly, too.   He was quite an
amateur cook, and one day made some splendid oyster stew; but it did
not exactly suit his wife, and she expressed her disapprobation by
dropping a fork on the floor accidently.   That was enough; the good
natured man picked up a bowl; smash it went, then another, then
a plate smash! then a cup, saucer, dish; then the cruet bottles.   His
wife did not attempt to stop him, but when he was through she laughed
at him; he snatched his hat in fury and rushed to the door.   His wife
had hard work to coax him to return and eat his dinner, but for months
he took his bread and milk out of the butter dish—his wife would buy
no more bowls!   Another time he thought he would cook some savory
sausages.   His wife, being hungry, cooked one while he was preparing.

If a thunderbolt had shattered the house, if a water spout had burst
and drowned them all, if an earthquake had shook them through to
China, she could not have been more surprised than at the vial of
wrath that burst upon her head!   The husband almost danced with
anger.

''Yes! I've seen it for some time; I don't suit you any more!''

"Why, Pet! I was so hungry!''

''Thunderation!''   Smash went the stove-lifter—broke!   ''I know
—nothing I do suits you these days,'' etc.

After the husband had finished explaining himself, and his wife
wanted to explain also, he went for the street—that's the way some of
us escape it—and his wife had to coax and plead to get him back to
his sausages and his senses.   See the cause he had!   Why did his
wife not wait and eat with gentility, and—a knife and fork, instead of
seizing a broiling hot sausage in her fingers, as if she was starved?

It is only in such extreme cases that we have the weakness to use
a woman's weapon, *the tongue.*

I hope I've proved to you that we men don't scold, or if we do,
our actions speak so much louder than our words, that we get the

reputation of being, perhaps, a little more *angelic* than we really are. But you ladies, being naturally sweet and weak, and not of deter‐ mined action, overflow with words, and are therefore called by the peculiar name of scolds!

Take my advice, practice with dumb-bells, war-clubs, boxing‐ gloves, the Health Lift—anything to develop your muscle, remember‐ ing always that actions speak louder than words! Be advised.

And this is how May's husband acted.

Hop-O'-My-Thumb.

ON THE WAR PATH.

The subjoined "talk" comes from a lady friend who attended the lecture of Ingersoll, and there learned to talk back. She is getting in‐ dependent, speaks of herself as a full partner in the firm matrimonial, and believes she is as much entitled to have a good time as her hus‐ band has to play Blue Peter and cinch at the club. We are not re‐ sponsible for the views of our (lady) correspondents:

I have been trying for a few weeks Woman's Natural Sphere, with not a thought above cleaning pots and pans, and what should compose the next dinner. My knees have been bent more to the God of Clean‐ liness than for many a long day to the God of Love. The lamp has been filled and the fleas brushed away, and yet I have failed to dis‐ cover that it is at all elevating or soul inspiring, or that your husband loves you two cents more for being the family drudge. And I have come to the conclusion that it is by no means an intelligent woman's sphere, no matter how much bosh a man may write about it, and that your children think less of "mamma," with soiled hands and drabbled dress, than when she is singing in the parlor, or even writing trash for the newspapers, and yet I am not " strong minded," and don't want to vote—at least till the next election.   My hands feel as if, instead of 5¾, I could easily wear 7½, Jouvin's best; and instead of 1½ ankle ties, the shoes of the Chinese Giant would be more comfortable.   I have broken my corset lace, and ruined my " pinback," and all that my beloved should smoke fine cigars, and play " Pedro" for the drinks, and now I've *done*.   I'm going to hire a Dutch girl as strong

as an ox, and big enough to keep the family straight.   When dinner is ordered for six P. M., we have dinner at six P. M., if there is only an old hat to sit in the chair opposite me for company. I have learned in these few weeks of stern experience that a woman is a f——, excuse me, an angel, to work and worry her life out, because she happens to be a partner in a firm, the

This is the Hat.

other half of which spends all the money and has all the fun, she getting her board and lodging, like any other servant, without a "thank you," for all her trouble, and the house being ever so clean, whereas, a " hired lady help," would be spoken to softly with praise for the scrubbed floor, and nice dinner, and a convenient little twenty-dollar gold piece at the end of the month; and yet they are not happy, and if they are not kissed behind the door, they soon seek fresh fields and pastures new.

Well, well, well! Will no experience teach a woman how to manage a husband? I have had experience, years of experience, and yet I am as far from the goal as ever, and have come to the conclusion that unless a man has the bumps of time and order well developed, that a woman wastes her time in trying to be either a good house-keeper or a good husband-tamer; and my advice is, find out where those bumps or deficiencies are, and go for them.

P. S. You think I am trying to make women discontented (so I am) with their mamby-pamby—work-themselves-gray—lives. Let them rise up in their might and dignity, and show a man he is not *everybody;* that there is such a thing as a woman to be considered, who is now going to take her place as joint-head of the house, which he will soon learn to his utter amazement. Oh! don't think that this is my experience; do not give me the discredit of being such a simpleton; but a lady friend whispered it in my ear, and if it is her experience, it is the experience of thousands of others; for there is no blessed or unblessed exception that elevates one woman to the extreme hights of happiness, and depresses another to the lowest depths of misery—it runs pretty even, and woman is only woman all the world over.

And this is what Agnes says.

PUNCTUALITY.

Some men are not punctual. We revere our sex, still, we are not blind, like love, so we see the few faults that are hardly discernable in that perfection of humanity—a man.

Perhaps it would be better for our own sake that we cultivate this quality, habit, characteristic, or what it may be called. First and foremost, we should hear sweeter music in our mother tongue, syllabled by our wife.

The moments slip by so rapidly when one is just finishing a war-story, or is deep in a discussion as to the relative merits of the rival Presidential candidates; and we are reasonably surprised when we are a little late, say fifty or sixty minutes, to meet a small-sized thundercloud at the door.

"Where have you been?"

"Why, what time is it, dear?"

"An hour past dinner-time, and everything is spoiled."

"Really, I must take my watch to the jeweler's"—taking it out. "Why, it is five o'clock by this, and you say I'm an hour late Then this must be much too slow!"

This excuse will only do occasionally, as it soon becomes monotonous and thin, and dinner-time is too early to mention Lodge. That has to bear enough for itself and fifty other things, when night comes.

This is the Business.

So when we wish to watch the pretty girls coming from the matinees, we have to invent, and our brain must be fertile if we often wish for meeting an old friend or a spendid customer—can't be repeated too often, if our wives have the penetration and appreciaton we gave them credit for when they chose us. Besides, they know about what time our business ends for the day.

Sometimes we can put it on the cars, and happy is the man who can plead a car off the track or a fractious horse.

But why the women act as if life and death depended upon one being home at just such a time, we cannot see.

What if dinner is a little overdone, so long as it is hot and served with mild words, it will taste well enough.

I know a wife who once took the notion into her head to always wait dinner for her lord. The first month she went hungry ; the second, cross; the third, nearly starved the children; the fourth was furious; the fifth, tried to hunt him up; the sixth, *ate dinner without him*, and there was peace and quietness all around; the children were satisfied, the servants stopped their grumbling, and the wife, not being hungry and tired with waiting, was in a better humor and inclined to look more leniently on the causes of the delay.

This I would advise all our wives to do, 'after waiting a reasonable length of time, say half to two hours; this is about as much as any woman's patience can stand, or their appetites either.

We know that we are so fascinating, that it is hard to eat without us, and we should be really pleased and flattered, if it were some one else's wife waiting for us so anxiously ; but being ours, it is an old story, and we are apt to be angry when they complain of hunger.

"Why don't you eat, then? I have told you to a hundred times. I wouldn't go hungry, I can tell you, with a good dinner waiting."

"But it is so lonely to eat without you—I see so little of you, that I scarcely get a chance to talk to you any more."

"Oh, fudge!"

You see, it doesn't do to be too romantic after being married a couple of years or so. We know that this thinking too much of us, waiting for our coming, and watching for our smiles, is apt to make a woman look old and worn ; so take my advice, ladies, and *don't do it*.

I wan't to whisper something, so that my brothers shan't hear; bend down your head: We don't think near so much of you for it—be a little more devil and less angel, and you will hold us to you the stronger.

I heard the wife of a friend of mine once say to him:

"If I was a man, I wouldn't trust you one bit in a business matter, because you never keep your word."

He laughed pleasantly, and replied :

"Oh, it's nothing to break your word to your wife; but in business it's a very different matter."

A friend of mine, whose dinner-hour is six, strolled in at eight one evening, with a friend whom he had brought home to dinner. The inconsiderate wife had dined without him.

"I'm afraid I've kept your husband a little late," said the guest.

He got an emphatic reply in the shape of the scrag end of the joint and cold vegetables.

Some of us think, no matter what time we drop in for dinner, it should be done to a turn; and I have heard some men scold—excuse me—express their mind freely, when dinner had waited two or three hours and was not quite so good as if just served up, that their wives were no housekeeper, and couldn't cook like their mother!

These gentlemen should have a series of dinners—or, rather, their wives should attend to it—like Cleopatra did when she was entertaining Antony ; so, if they were not ready for one when it was cooked, several more would be forthcoming.

Hop-O'-My-Thumb.

And this is the attention Lizzie received from her husband.

ABOUT HUSBANDS' PRESENTS.

So you didn't even thank your husband for his beautiful present? A diamond ring, too; because he could not come to bring you home the very day he promised?

Oh, you goose! Husbands give presents too rarely for them to be treated lightly. Take advice from one who is older in experience of husbands than you are and don't do so any more. Do you know what he told me quietly?—that it would be a long time before you got another.

Now, what I say I say freely and without prejudice, both to you and my other dear friends. Accept any and every present your husband gives, always with smiles, always with thanks; praise the gift, if you can one-twentieth part conscientiously, or admire the great taste displayed in selecting it; go into raptures over it, if it is in the least a rapture-inspiring gift. Depend upon it, you'll get many, very many more by this simple process, than by "Oh, how ugly! What did you buy that for? I needed shoes so much more. You men don't know how to buy anything. Why didn't you give me the money?'"

"What taste! Why the pattern is only fit for a bed quilt! They've cheated you; you've paid twice too much for it."

Now, this hurts their self-opinion, and what husband in the face of such talk—and my dear female friends, you know this is no fancy talk, but what you tell those poor Benedicks almost every present they give you—now what husband, I say, will be constantly bringing home little knicknacks, and you know very well, or perhaps you don't, that they will often buy little things for you, when they are pleasantly received, that you might live till the next Centennial and they'd never think of offering you the money to buy.

I know a lady whose husband returning from a long journey, brought his wife two dress patterns; one a silk—black, striped with yellow—the other, a kind of red damask. "Whew, how his wife will fret!" I thought, as he pulled them so tenderly from his valise and showed them to me so admiringly. What could I say? Well, I smiled and said they were very nice; so they were for some things; damask would make nice curtains, for example; the silk would pass if his wife had been a little gayer. She came to me not long after, with a sad, pitying smile on her face, and said:

"Look!"

"'Sh! Don't say anything against them; he showed them to me so proudly. The silk will look quite nicely made up."

"But look at the other, the one I wanted so; it looks like curtains or furniture covering."

"Why it will make a splendid morning dress. Don't show that they do not please you, or he never will bring anything the next time he has an opportunity." She took them sadly and went away, but to this day I never saw her wear them.

Now my beloved once bought me a collar among other really useful and pretty things. He said to the servants, triumphantly:

"You can't guess what that cost?"

Our new-made citizens of color grinned and said:

This is the Collar.

"Dunno, Curnel!" They take pride in titles.

"Well, for what I paid for this collar, you could buy two barrels of flour."

" De Lor' bress us!" and they gaped wide-mouthed looking upon it with almost awe.

Of course I was delighted, and thanked him kindly and gave him a kiss for all the pretty things he brought me ; then he told me how the lady had said what a good judge of laces he was; seldom men could tell so well, etc. I suppose she was young and pretty, but don't know—only she fooled my confiding darling most terribly—for the collar was imitation Valenciennes, sewed on by no means fine muslin garnished with two cherry satin bows. But I wore it, and though my lady friends knew it was not real, I never let him know, and he is in ignorance to this day, that he is not one of the finest judges of laces in the world.

I remember the first time he brought home a loaf filled with fried oysters; he had been out, and it was rather late, so I pouted at first, and wouldn't eat any; but he kept good-natured, ate some, and said 'Take some, Pet, they are splendid!' Well, after expressing my mind a little about late hours, etc., I did eat some, and they were splendid, so I finished them, and the natural suavity of my temper returned.

I found out that pouting and quarreling with the oysters did not keep him from going out when he wanted to, and only left me hungry to go to bed. I hinted for oysters next time. In Philadelphia they do them up in paper boxes and give them an expressive name, and more wives get fried oysters than they ever did before.

Never tell your husband he is wasting money when he brings you home a *petit souper*, or some nice strawberries, for depend upon it, if he don't bring them to you, he eats them himself, and how much better it would be to enjoy them with him, for he judges you by himself, thinking that you appreciate such things, and that good eating is one of the greatest pleasures of life; and after all, there is something in it, or it would never have become a proverb that " The way to a man's heart is through his stomach."

Oh, ladies, treat these little attentions kindly, or the day may come when you'll have no little attentions to treat any way at all. Sing to your husbands,

> Dearest love, now listen to me,
>   When you feel inclined to bring,
> Dress or collar, boots or stockings,
>   Or some less pretentious thing;
> Oh, bring your presents right along,
>   I will thank you with a kiss;
> Such attentions are so pleasing,
>   And so seldom—that 'tis bliss,
>   To be so honored.

HOP-O'-MY-THUMB.

SERVANT GIRLS.

Why our wives will persist in hiring those hideous China boys when there are so many nice girls to be had, is more than I can tell. Now I am a moral man, and twenty nice girls would not tempt me. But there are *pros* and *cons* to every question. I am on the *pro* side at present, but I have a friend who is on the *con* side, if that means against. He is a lean, cadaverous looking man, with weary eyes and a plaintive voice. One evening he was passing our door, so I asked him in, but my wife was sitting on the steps, looking smiling and pretty, so he shook his head with a sigh, and asked me if I would not walk a block or two with him ; my wife in pity, said, "yes, go," so I went. After walking a short distance in silence he began :

"It is a good thing to have a friend—one to whom you can confide your griefs, that, preying on you alone might make you misanthropic.

My friend, you are still young; your hair is brown and curly; let my appearance be a warning to you." He sighed and wiped his dewy brow with a large silk handkerchief.

"My wife is a good woman, but she employed a Chinaman, and my life was a misery ; food ill-cooked, shirts scorched and collars limp. I endured it like a good husband, till he took the size of the iron out of the bosom of my best shirt, then I mildly suggested to my wife that we had better try white help. I didn't say girl, so my wife said she'd see, and the next day there was a clean, tidy girl around the house."

"Your wife is a sensible woman," I remarked.

He gave me a sad look, with his weary blue eyes, and continued ; "You are right—we got along nicely for several days ; food well done, shirts perfection. This fact I remarked to my wife, saying how much pleasanter they were to wear, done up by clean, rosy fingers than by a Chinaman, whose work always made me feel uncomfortable. I did not then understand the peculiar look that gleamed in her eyes. I got up a little earlier than my wife, so Maria used to tell me 'good morning' very pleasantly; and as I sat doing my writing before breakfast, it was cheerful to see her smiling face pop in and out on various errands ; 'how should she cook this or that,' ' did I like my coffee strong,' etc. ; so we soon got well acquainted, but knowing my wife was particular I scarcely spoke to her when she was about. Our door had no key, and I suppose I used to forget to shut it tight, for the wind used to make it screak very often in the early morning. One night my wife gave me a severe lecture—I suppose I deserved it ; she went to sleep talking, and woke early and finished it, so I arose in not a very amiable temper toward her. Maria spoke to me kindly. 'Here,' thought I, 'is one who cares for me.' She looked so nice, too, that I suddenly snatched a kiss from her lips, and she as suddenly uttered a slight scream. The devil must have tempted me. Had ten tuns of dynamite been under the house, or a thousand pounds of nitroglycerine, with a hundred hammers playing Yankee Doodle on the

This is the Wig.

cans, or any thing that was terrible, dire, devastating, it could not equal the shock that disturbed our house. Well, Mária went to the hospital, and I wear a wig." Again he sighed, and I did not know how to comfort him.

"Yes, upon the whole," he said, "I think I would rather have the Chinaman ; they do not lead one into temptation, and my hair is getting a good chance to grow underneath the wig."

"My friend, you should have been a moral man, like me."

"I was tempted by Satan, but my wife is an exemplary woman; I only got my deserts, for should I catch her kissing a young man, there would be no need of hospitals or wigs ; a post-mortem would do them." Again he sighed, and wringing my hand, wended his way to his home. And I began to muse on the folly of men who neglected their lawful wives who endured pain, anguish, and many times deprivation for them, to kiss the servant girl. Depend upon it, Oh, foolish men, the servant girl whose lips are free to you, have been free to every man before you, who has been honored by her presence in his home.

Now, I am a moral man, yet I say that, to those of us who get up early, as many of us do, either from choice or necessity, the "yesee," "me no sabee," "belly good," in the harsh mongolian voice, and the sickly yellow skin, is not as conducive to digestion as our kindly mother tongue, and a rosy face and cleanly neck, surrounded by a white collar. But my wife who is an angel, says : "There is but one good man in the world, and each of us think we have him ; so, Pet, I won't place temptation in your way."

. "But, my dear, I'm a moral man, and not to be tempted." She laughed lightly, but *the China boy staid*. I know my wife ; though small, she has a large will of her own, and just enough devil in her—as well as angel—that if I were to look once too often at the same woman, let alone squeeze her hand or kiss her, that she would put miles, aye leagues, nay even the briny deep between us, and go home to her ma ! And who knows but she might leave me the nursing baby, too? I took care of that young hopeful, once, for just one half hour, while my wife went to a neighbor's to borrow a book. Shall I ever forget it? Never, no never ! I cannot describe in words what I suffered ; no, it is buried down deep in my heart, and never do I want even the memory of that half hour to be renewed, or even aroused again.

"My love," I ventured to say once more, "if you had a nice girl, she would take care of the baby, then you could enjoy yourself so much more."

But she shook her head, and her dark eyes sparkled merrily.

"Why, love, surely you don't think so little of yourself as to be jealous? How could I think of any one else, while you are so pretty and attractive ?"

"Well, I like my morning nap; I wouldn't care to have it disturbed even by tantalizing thoughts."

"What need would there be to be disturbed ?"

"Now, it is no use to talk, Pet. I know a little of human nature, and I wouldn't want to be tempted too far myself."

Good heaven! what did she mean ? What a storm of virtuous indignation I poured upon that devoted woman's head ! What ! could anything under the blue sky tempt her? I was horror-struck. I, myself, knew enough of human nature, to be aware of the fact that some men had their little weakness ; thank heaven not me ! But that a woman— demure, sensible, sensitive little woman, should acknowledge to her own lord and master, that she did not consider herself invulnerable to all the temptations that all the world could bring against her, sent me into a cold perspiration. When I could get breath from the exhaustion produced by the severity of the rebuke I gave her, I said with calmness and manly dignity :

"Oh, keep your Chinaman ; but never let such words fall from your lips again, Madame ! " So the China boy remains till this day,

Hop-O'-My-Thumb.

And this is what Kate's husband says.

——

WHAT SHALL WE DO WITH OUR WIVES ?

"Only one hour a day, Pet,"

"You have house, servant, and children to look after; that's enough to occupy your time."

"There's only ladies in the class I want to join, and it's very cheap."

"Put such thoughts from your mind ; you have no time for painting and such stuff."

The wife turned away with a sigh, and the husband went to his daily occupation. Now do you know that husband was a — — well, something that is best expressed by two dashes.

So the wife washes the baby, puts him to bed for his morning nap, darns a pair of Pet's stockings, gives directions for dinner, and then— well the day is so lovely and her hat so becoming, that she'll just take a little walk down town. There she meets an old beau, for where one is brought up, you know, there is always one or two old sweethearts lyiñg around. How strange! He also has an errand on that very street, so they walk and talk, and the time passes right merrily. So when she goes home to her solitary lunch, she has something to occupy her thoughts—not exactly what her husband wishes, still she is not littering the house up with her accomplishments; and as he does not know of her accidental walks and talks, he is all serene.

Now when I marry, my wife may make a brick yard of the kitchen, and a paint shop of the parlor; but I'll keep her thoughts and heart to myself, even at the price of seeing her Pet—that's your humble servant—reproduced in sickly looking plaster, or staring out of very open eyes from a canvas, and the little Pets ditto. The first is easily knocked down and smashed, and made fit for the ash barrel, or broken, so that she has a month's work to put it together again, and the second soon can find its way to the garret.

. We forget, we men, that while our lives are busy with a constant variety, our wives' are an even monotone; while we see a thousand faces on the street or in the office, they see the baby's and the China boy's, with perhaps a couple of callers during the week. Is it a wonder that they chat with the butcher, the baker, the candle-stick maker, and even the oysterman, for variety's sweet sake? If we take away all their intellectual employment, what shall they do? When the house is in order, the children attended to, the last borrowed book read, and nothing to sew, *what shall they do?* They can't be making baby clothes all the time, for but few of them have purses of their own, unless they deal in stocks ; and you wouldn't like them to cut holes in your best coat to have something to sew, would you, now? They can't—figuratively speaking— roll themselves up in leaves and spin their lives out, like silk worms, for some one else's use, can they? I know a poor lady who occupies her time in constantly changing the position of the furniture ; so her home is always in a muddle, and she has a far-away, dreamy look in her eyes. Now if she only knew how to enlarge her sphere of action, she might become a valuable member of society. But her husband don't believe in woman's rights and won't tell her what to do, so I suppose she'll continue changing the furniture till she goes where there's no furniture to change.

You don't come home till six o'clock, and the day is very long, and sometimes very weary with nothing to do. Let her write, if only once a year some paper condescends to accept an article, and most of her beautiful thoughts become the property of the rag man at so much per pound; what of that? It keeps her at home, and busy, and improves her mind a little, if you care at all for that.

Now I have a friend who has a real charming little wife, whom he leaves with a kiss at breakfast, when he don't forget it, and does not see her again until six at night. He does not ask her what she has been doing all day, or appear at all interested how she passes the time, if the dinner is good and the house clean, all his buttons on, and no holes in his stockings. He tells her a trifle of what is going on down town; not often until he is asked, though, and being tired, in a little while he goes to bed; and if friends call, they have to whisper out of the window, to wait a moment as they are just putting the children in their little bed; and such a hurrying and scurrying on of pants, boots and petticoats as you never saw.

These are the Children

Now, how can a woman be a companion and helpmeet to a man if he won't let her?—and he is only a type of thousands of others—especially when they wish to deprive these poor women of everything but housekeeping! Good gracious! she can't be thinking of something to eat all the time, neither can she be constantly washing the little faces, until the turn-up noses are red, and the eyes full of tears. Ah! but she has one outlet—glorious, satisfying, piquant—gossip! Oh! woman's friend! How many weary hours do you fill of that vapid life? How many a wrinkle do you prevent coming on that face, still young, that otherwise would be brooding at home, fancying itself ill-used?

All hail to thee, Gossip! and thy kindly uses, hid from the eyes of the vulgar many; but revealed to those who need thee most!

Well, then, what shall we do with our wives? Give them plenty of newspapers, and, books too, when you can afford them; let them dabble in paint, or mudddle in clay; write poetry or prose; go to the matinee; or, better still, take them at night—there is less temptation to flirt. Don't always go to bed at eight o'clock, but play a game of cards or chess, or bring home a friend once in a while to spend an evening and break the, to you, monotony of seeing only one face for a whole half hour. Tell her she looks nicely, when you see she has tried to please you, and don't be praising somebody else before her face. Remember she has feelings—if she did marry you. Treat her a little as you wish to be treated yourself; and don't forget to give her some pocket-money, for how would we like to be constantly without a cent in our purse, and not even a car ticket to pay for a ride?

Yours in adversity,

Hop-O'-My-Thumb.

And this is little Pet's—Morgan's wife's—secret.

DARNING STOCKINGS.

"Sweet Rebecca, charming maid,
Darning stockings in the shade."

That's the way the poet has it.

Pouting wife all in a flury,
Darning stockings in a hurry,
Not darning in poetic shade,
But 'darning' all bad hose that's made.

That's the way we have it. Why will husbands persist in wearing nails in the inside, instead of the outside of their boots? Why will they endure the penance of Saint Somebody, who had to wear peas in his shoes, just to give us poor wives the pleasant torture of mending their stockings. It is so easily said:

"There, — it, I've no clean stockings!" But a hole as big as the top of your baby's head, is not so easily mended, and if we do take the advantage of mending the stockings with the smallest holes first, it is not becoming a loving husband to object to wear odd ones, even if one is a little thicker than the other. Can't they make a little concession to the tender sex? They grant it so often in politics and business, to the opposite ditto. Or why not petition the manufacturers to make

These are the Socks.

them all alike, except in size? Then you see we could throw away the ones with the big, big holes, and not feel so guilty as we would destroying a pair.

"Sweet Rebecca!" Here we have a picture of a lovely girl, with delicate white hands, and slender fingers, that never burned themselves with pot or pan, or stove-lifter; her dress trim and pretty, her apron white, not having wiped the bottom of hot dishes, to preserve the purity of the table cloth. "Charming maid!" Knowing not yet the maternal occupation of attending to the wants of nine small children; nine little faces to wash and heads to comb; eighteen little hands to scour, and thirty-six little shoes and stockings to put on, lace and tie, and eighty-one buttons to button. And this all expected to be done in ten minutes and three-quarters. Ah! innocent Rebecca, do not add this experience too soon, but keep to your darning stockings in the shade, with the sunlight just gilding your hair; the birds singing, the sweet grass kissing your shoe. The work in your hand, perhaps your own fair hose, that has lovingly encased your dear little foot and—leg —or, 'tis perhaps a lover's sock knit by your fair hand, and 'tis but pleasure to mend the slight abrasions caused by the pressure of his loved, manly foot. Dream on, fair maid, till the reality of

Great big holes in stockings many,
Little time, and scarcely any
Inclination for the pastime,
Vowing each shall be the last time,
That you will spend your strength and time,
In darning socks not worth a dime.
With cotton coarse, and needle small,
That scarcely will go through at all;
More you pull, the more it tangles,
In your mind with words it jangles;
When at last you stick your finger,
O'er that sock no more you'll linger.
Though I know 'tis very shocking,
You're apt to say "d— that stocking,"

Awakes you, alas! it will come too soon, and with it, perhaps, a
frowsy head and slip-shod shoes, and a husband who reads the paper
at breakfast, and blacks his boots on the kitchen table!

This is no woman's secret, we only wish it was.

"DANIEL DERONDA."

Hop-O'-My-Thumb's Opinion.

Book of many wishes! How I saved up my pennies, as it were,
to purchase it.   When I read that the author had already received the
sum of eighty thousand dollars as royalty, the book being sold in
England in eight parts, at five shillings per part, the author receiving
one pound on each book sold, I hardly think such a thing was ever
heard of before.   My desire to read it was even stronger a few days
after, when the sum reached two hundred thousand dollars and it was
still marching on, leaving every known writer far in the rear.   I determined, whether or no, to make Mr. "Deronda's" acquaintance—to
see him, talk with him, find out what was so wonderful about him,
that he should have taken the country, of dear books and not universal
reading, by storm.

'Twas night, and by the feeble light of a street car lamp I unwrap-
ped my little green and gold treasure.   What did I care if my fellow
travelers thought I was trying to appear the pedant; what I had wished
for so long couldn't be enjoyed too soon.   I passed my hand caress-
ingly over the neat binding, enjoying the sweet anticipation of what
was to come, a moment longer, then opened it.

" Man can do nothing without the make-believe of a beginning.

Even science, the strict measurer, is obliged to start with a make-be-lieve unit, and must ˏfix on a point in the stars' unceasing journey when his sidereal clock shall pretend that time is at naught."

This is what first met my eyes, and it continued at some length in the same style. ''Ah!'' I thought, "this is a book to improve one; the headings are so fine—a little mystical and obtuse, requiring study, but perhaps that is so much the better." Then I began the story. It opens in a German gambling saloon; the heroine, Gwendolen, an English girl, at one of the tables. Now, to me, there is something un-natural and repulsive in a young girl, especially an English girl, as a centre object in such a scene. I was disappointed, and the further I read my disappointment did not decrease till I came to near the end of the book. Vol. I. Gwendolen is unloving and unlovable. I scarcely care what becomes of her. The description of her person does not at all coincide with what she really is. I use the ego so much because this is the opinion of but one person; as yet I have met no one who has read the book, but those that have may consider it '' grand,'' as a lady told me she heard it was; but I shall take no one's word and follow, as we are apt to do, either in art or books, some one else's lead, as we did in childhood with '' Follow my Lady Tipsy Toe.'' I know I run the risk of being considered conceited, setting myself up, and everything that's disagreeable, if I have an opinion of my own, and that opinion is different from that of the many. But I never could say an Old Master was superb when I thought it was hideous.

The first part of the book is very English, with the nobility, the Archery meetings, and the grand parks. It does not come home to the heart; that is why I cannot imagine how the book could have had such a wonderful sale.

Her sketches of thought-life are very good, but often so deep and complicated that they are about as easily understood as Greek or Hebrew, to one who knows neither of these languages, and has only a part of a dictionary to help them.

For instance, is not this hard to understand ?   Is it not a little too deep and far-fetched ?   And the book is full of such :

"Yet how distinguish what our will may wisely save in its completeness from the heaping of cat-mummies and the expensive cult of enshrined putrefactions ?"

Every chapter, too, has a heading about as obtuse as this.

I thought a book to be popular must touch the universal heart, must be so imbued with sympathy for suffering, must so scarify hypocrisy and evil-doing that their hideousness would disgust rather than fascinate ; or that some vital question of the present must be so presented and discussed, that we poor plodders would be shown the right way, and helped up to a higher plane.   But none of these elements struck me in my coveted book.   When "Deronda" is fully introduced, a little of human sympathy is aroused ; we can easily think that something is going to happen between himself and Gwendolen in the next volume, (which is not yet out.)   But she must prove very different from what she is at present for any one to care very much ; for a woman who would deliberately marry a man who has a left-handed wife, and several beautiful children, and is not only warned, but sees them, and although she flies from him, the minute poverty comes, she accepts him very complacently, with not a stir of passion in her heart to justify her.   Then, when she gets another letter, just after her marriage, only telling her what she already knew, she shrieks in terror at her husband's approach, we consider her not only a very foolish girl, but almost criminally weak.   When Myrah comes on the scene, together with the Mayricks, we begin to feel we are with a human family again, somewhat like people we have known.

I expect to like the second volume very much more than the first, for I anticipated something so different, which not getting—human-like—I would not be satisfied with, and perhaps did not appreciate what I did get.

FASHIONABLE.

Now, we like to be fashionable; we don't particularly mind the stings and arrows that outrageous editors hurl against us, provided the fashion becomes us. We know that the side views, or, to speak artistically, the profiles of some of our lady acquaintances were rather on the comical order when the hair was worn high, and the hat on the furthest top of the aforesaid, so we avoided the extreme of fashion, although by doing so, we might as well have been out of world, according to the old saying. So we thought we'd take an intermediate position, somewhere between the earth and space, and wear our hair not so high and our hat further on our head. How the ladies could see each other at church and at the theatre, and observe the grotesqueness of the fashionable hair and head gear, then go and do likewise, we never could tell, unless their idea was to be in the fashion if they dyed for it, which they very soon did, and now we have a race of blondes. We rather liked that color, and begged our lord and master to let us "blonde" a little; but his "no" was so stern and determined, that being a little woman and weak we didn't dare to disobey. True, we might have been like one pretty young lady here, who blonded so much, or so suddenly that all her hair came out, and now she wears a wig! *Sic transit gloria mundi*—or rather in this case—hair dye.

So we bought a military chapeau, that came well on our head and was quite stylish, but rather large ; but we thought it was *the* hat of the city, till we got tired of it. Excuse the numerous "we ;" but little people always were the most conceited people in the world, thinking their diminutive individuality equal to several of a larger growth.

Ah! how well we remember our first pull-back! We thought it the smoothest, tightest of any yet out. What though we could only sit on the extreme edge of the car seat, it made us an object of interest, and we liked that, although our back did ache a little, and when we landed our steps had to be very short and "pit-i-pat !" But what was our horror to discover tighter and smoother ones than ours mincing along the streets ; showing shape and avoirdupois, and all the graceful outline of the female form divine! We went home and loosened that pull-back. If we could not be first we would at least be comfortable. We know of but one concession being made to a pull-back that was of benefit to the wearer of aforesaid. A street-car conductor generously remitted the fine—excuse us—didn't take the fare of a young person whose long and tight P. B. would not allow her to get to her pocket, being encumbered with a sleeping child.

What is the use of you gentlemen railing against the styles ; you know you always do, no matter what they are; and yet you like a lady to be fashionable, and would rather take a dozen to the theatre dressed in the extreme, than one attired in the fashion of a few years ago, when an immense hoop was all the rage. Whew ! how people would stare at one now.

But the happy medium in fashions, as in most other things, is always the best and most comfortable ; but it is not every one who has the nerve to act for themselves. Cultivate your nerves, ladies, cultivate them, and the result will help you along in this world wonderfully.

We know a young person whose husband invited her for a short walk, and the minute she appeared on the street, where it would have been rather inconvenient to have made a change of dress, he complained of her attire, saying :

"You look like the Witch of Endor ! Is that the way you go down town ?" She replied meekly, "I did not know you wished me to put on

This is the Shawl.

my best, as we are only going on an errand to the grocery. It would have taken me some little time to do so ; this is the only shawl I have, and it is quite cold." It was a red affair, with a huge pattern, that he himself had bought her, her taste rather revolting at it, at the time, she knowing it would be the only one for the next ten years. "Then you should not complain of my clothes, without putting your hand into your pocket and giving me the wherewithal to buy better. One cannot be fashionable on nothing." The smile that spread over his face was childlike and bland, and the discussion ended.

At another time ;

"Why can't you fix yourself as nicely as when Mrs. ——helped you ?" This time it was the lady's face that had the smile childlike and bland, for she knew the distinguished looking white veil, satin sacque, and light kids belonged to the aforesaid Mrs. ——It seemed so strange to her, that her husband should imagine ladies' finery dropped from the clouds, color and fit adapted. Did he get his boots and trousers that way, with maybe his tobacco thrown in ? It would seem that many men do, for they are sarcastic and complaining, thinking, no doubt, that words and wishes will make garments, without the small items of materials and dressmakers ; but it would be cool clothing for some climates. Venus rising out of the sea is all very beautiful and clasical, but would you like to see your dear little wife with only a petticoat of the clinging drops of the briny deep, and a pull-back of the foam of the mighty wave? Guess not, muchly.

This is what Frank's wife told me.

HOP-O'-MY-THUMB.

A WOMAN'S EXPOSÉ OF THE MALE HOUSE-KEEPER.

We send missionaries to the Fiji Islands; we send missionaries to the black Africans; we even try to civilize poor Lo, yet we pass with calm non-intervention the victim of worse than heathen barbarity, of worse than Indian deviltry—the wife of the male house-keeper. How tame these words to express her utter nonentity. Hidden in them lies to the one who has "been there" a world of degradation and unhappiness! If a man only knew how his wife suffered mentally, physically and in her very womanhood, by this detention of the household purse, the coin will burn his heart as well as hand.

" My dear, have you not a grocery-book, and is our credit not good at the butcher's? What can I do more? I'm sure the children's clothes are warm, if they are plain." Thus he talketh and thinketh he doeth his duty.

The milk man comes.

"When can you pay that little bill?" but as neither the grocer's book, nor your credit at the butcher's, provides for this contingency, you can only tell him to "call again;" so he continues to call till his bill becomes long and his patience short; and if you get the money any sooner than your husband thinks it right and proper he should wait, you do it by absolute quarreling, and it is as grudgingly given as if it were for the most useless luxury, as if he did not drink it in his coffee, in his whisky and with his bread.

Then John Chinaman brings home the necessary weekly linen.

"Pay next weekee, John." You can't always make John understand this, and so are edified by several visits, till you talk the money out of your husband in sheer desperation. The dry goods you can get at the grocer's you are welcome to; but as that generally amounts to needles, cotton and shirt buttons, with, may-be, hairpins and braid, your chances for a Summer dress are t. t.—terribly thin—and you are told you don't "fix up" like you did before your marriage, but the hand never goes into the pocket to give you the wherewithal to obtain the much desired end. You are twitted with not being stylish, and you haven't seen a new dress for more than a year except on somebody else, perhaps your "lady help," for she can dress in style, the male house-keeper having to pay *her* whether stocks are up or down, or business bad or good. Perhaps you take an economical fit and do the work, your d. h. (that's "dear husband") promises to pay you instead of the aforesaid "help" thereby saving the keep of one; but at the end of the month he has forgotten his promise, and says he

CAN'T AFFORD IT!

When the grocer has no needles, pins and stamps, you are in a terrible fix. The "news" in your letters becomes "olds," lying on the mantle-piece waiting for the portrait of the Father of his Country to be affixed thereon, and as for pins, how are the young ladies to pin up the holes in their stockings without them? I've seen two do it, and the other day a lady I know hunted all over her five rooms on hands and knees to find a needle to sew a button on her husband's shirt. She spent an hour and a half of time and then only succeeded in finding a poor, miserable, crooked one that had never been lost, and too small at that; so she had to take her fortune—twenty-five cents that lay concealed in her best dress pocket—and sally forth to purchase some. The tears nearly came to her eyes, to think that she had to demonetize this huge piece of silver, the like of which she did not expect soon to see again, except in broker's windows; but the husband's buttons must be sewed on, if banks break!

"My dear, I must have some money ; there is no use talking."

"Oh, don't bother me about money. I'm sick of the subject."

"BUT THE CHILDREN'S CLOTHES—"

"That'll do. I hate almost to come into the house." Then he slams the door and goes and consoles himself at the corner, playing for the cigars, and loses fifty cents to a dollar, and considers it nothing, for it goes on the book ; and the end of the month is no better than the beginning to the wife of the male house-keeper. The children go in patched and repatched rags, and the wife wears her Winter bonnet in the scorching July sun, till it makes her head ache. Women don't like to ask and ask and ask for every little article of clothing, till they feel as if they were the poorest and most importunate of beggars, so they look dowdy, and their underclothes leave them by peacemeal, and still the male housekeeper is blind. "I buy so much better meat than you do," he says, with pride, forgetting that if by chance he gives her the market money, once in an age, he expects her to make it go twice as far as he does. I know a gentleman who cannot make twenty-five dollars a week keep his house, but is going to be generous and let his wife try and do it with ten! No knocking down in that house for pull-backs of five cent calico, or six-bit hats, or the unheard of luxury of a Saturday matinee. It's pinch and contrive and hunt, but never cajole. Most women are too proud, thank Heaven, for that. The male housekeeper is always the man who has

A GROCERY BOOK,

The Book.

That curse of a small salary; that curse to economy; that precursor to the poor-house ! Oh! why cannot these liquor-selling, gambling corner groceries be supressed! They are the causes of more divorces, more separations, more female infidelities than all the incompatibilities of temper the world over. Men will not be warned till it is too late. A lady friend of mine who, a few years ago, was living in loving happiness with her husband, startled me with the news of her divorce. " It began in the corner groceries," she said, and thousands can truthfully say the same. Because a woman joins her destiny to a man from pure love, leaving a happy home and loving friends, is it right, that after the first three days he should shamefully neglect her for the miserable, common trash that loaf about a corner grocery ? Is it right that she shall stay in the house, not home, without her husband, alone and silent, shedding bitter tears and thinking dangerous thoughts till 12, till 1, nay, sometimes till 2 strikes from the ghostly clock ? When a man has several small children, he knows his wife is so tied down that she cannot resent his insulting indifference without outraging her mother love, so he takes his cue accordingly, and neglects her to his heart's content, not caring that she grows thin, and pale, and old, and haggard ; not caring that she almost prays for death to release her from the sufferings of a seemingly unloved wife. So the male housekeeper keeps his grocery book and his butcher's book, and his house looks neglected and poverty stricken—no pictures, no ornaments, no books, he's sick of such nonsense—his children are poorly dressed, his wife ditto, and he always in debt, paying more for what he gets, purchasing what he cannot afford, treating old bummers to drinks and cigars, so generous, and still spends more than his wife would, making the house bright and pleasant, herself and children lovable with pretty clothes, and every bill paid—all to be a male housekeeper !

TIGER

(In the cause of women).

Several women's secret.

————

THE WRONG WROUGHT BY A CORNER GROCERY.

*   *   *   *   *   *

I never wrote an article for a paper in my life, but I have been tempted many times to do so, and after carefully reading the article in your Ladies' Column this morning, in regard to "corner groceries" and male "house-keepers," I made up my mind that for once, I would say a few words thereto, indorsing every sentiment.   I have been suffering for fourteen years from the corner groceries, and if I had the power to suppress the awful evil there should not one remain to tell the story.   In all these years I never possessed a pocket-book, never bought an article of dress, never had a half or a quarter of a dollar unless I earned it myself; and when I did receive my salary, it was borrowed, but never returned in a single instance.   I looked up to my husband as the provider, and felt I must carefully keep the house in order and do my work and sew for my family, and ask no questions. Years bring experience, and a person, if he have any sense at all, must see sometime that this is not the life intended by our Heavenly Father for intelligent beings.   The wife is never consulted, as she cannot understand business. (There is truth in that, too; one-sided business never suits an intelligent woman who lives to advance goodness, charity and purifications of all evils that are ready to spring up in a night). My belief of the married relation is, that if two are one by Divine order, then one is the companion of the other, and not one the servant and one the commander. Oh; how true it is in such a relation that the corner grocer's bill is the result! I am one of many who have had brown hairs prematurely sprinkled with gray, and wrinkles deeply set before youth had fairly reached its maturity. My husband could not afford to subscribe for a daily paper—at a salary of $150 per month—so he must necessarily go to the corner night after night.

This is the Corner Grocery.

Unsuspectingly I saw him go for years, and night after night I placed my house in order and the little ones to rest, and when quiet reigned I sat and sewed and mended, and thought how strangely different my life was from what I expected it to be. I gave him all the love that a true woman had to bestow, and I think he loved me in his way, and thought he was doing a husband's duty. But, oh, how it differed from mine or any other true woman's idea of love and wifely treatment! The end came at last, and the result was the inevitable one, of course—poverty and debt; and he escaped to a foreign land to die by his own hand from remorse, leaving wife and children to the mercy of creditors, and to bear the shame of years, of a past mis-spent in the corner groceries, playing for drinks and cigars. I have not magnified my wrongs; I could fill pages, but that would not suffice. This is a subject that should not be dropped in one hour. Will not some one continue to write with a pen of *fire* and place this awful evil in its true light, and take up the thread that "Tiger" has laid down, and never cease to tell all the evils attending the corner groceries and the card table, and bars concealed behind the lattice door, the open sesame of all family discord ?   TIGRESS.

This was written by some one unknown to the author, in answer to the foregoing.

GEORGE'S WIFE'S OPINION ON BOOKS.

I was sitting in my office—you, no doubt, think by this time I need a new bifurcated garment, sitting so much, but the fact is, a person does not consume so much oxygen in this sedentary occupation, as when exercising the pedestrian qualifications, and as free lunches necessitate ten to fifteen cent investments, and sometimes being out of such small amounts—I sit, and button my coat up as tightly as possible, not having a belt to use as the Indians do, when their larder is *nihil*—this is explanatory merely, so I'll continue—thinking about the advisability of writing a triumphant ode, now that the election is over and the country safe, but soon the sad fact occured to my mind, that poetry is rarely paid for by newspaper men, and although it is the dessert after the feast of substantial facts, still they think the glorification of seeing one's name in print is sufficient reward, when I was interrupted by the agreeable sound of George's wife's footsteps. She is always welcome, for her pleasant chat makes me forget, for the time, my troubles; then, too, she does not come so often as to wear her welcome out and also exhaust her conversational subjects.

"Come in, my dear," I cried, opening the door with alacrity.

"Uncle John, I'm so glad to see you! You are the only one to whom I can go when I am in trouble, or have a knotty point to settle; and do you know I've made a discovery?" she said, sinking into my big leather chair, to which I had led her.

"A Discovery?" I said, pulling up my paper collar, and running my fingers through my hair.

"And I've come to talk with you about it while it is fresh in my mind."

Visions of a splendid royalty in some grand beneficial invention, which I should help put on the high road of success, flitted through my mind, when Louisa again spoke.

"Yes, I've discovered, Uncle John, that all books are immoral!"— I looked at the young thing in horror; was she losing her senses?

"That is, most of them, and I've come to the conclusion that they are not much of a success unless they are."

"Louisa!" I said, reprovingly, thinking that marriage must have had a very bad effect on her.

"Oh! I don't mean with me, Uncle John, but with the great enlightened public. It seems strange too, for if we married women did half the wicked things the pet heroines of the successful books do, wouldn't the divorce courts be busy, and wouldn't the lawyers become nabobs for wealth! In France, of course, its different, if the stories told of that delightful country are true. Why, I read of a certain Countess who spent all her days in deeds of charity and missions of mercy, the aspect of demure innocence, yet her nights were riotous with licentious dissipation, she was the gayest of the gay and the wickedest of the wicked, yet when she was arrested she had dozens of offers of marriage, some saw so much romance—I don't fancy they could see much to love—in the two lives of the beautiful fiend."

"But that has nothing to do with books, my dear," I said gently, trying to bring her back to the subject. "Our own fireside Dickens, you, of course, except him?"

"Indeed I don't. Let us begin at any of his most popular works, say David Copperfield, for instance. There's little Em'ly; he had to make her bad to render her interesting, no'. bad in heart, but bad in act, and poor Martha was a few steps lower down the ladder. Then 'Dombey and Son,' though Mrs. Dombey was not frail, still she was a runaway wife. In this, too, he pictures a poorer sister, wretched and bad, though handsome and interesting—unfortunate Alice. If the heroine doesn't happen to be bad, then one of the principal personages must be, or the book is weak, lacks fire and so forth. Look at beloved Goethe. I get so angry at him, especially in his affinity piece, that I would like to read him a moral lecture, could he be induced to appear at some circle or cabinet seance. Why, one would think in reading him, I mean his writings, that it was absolutely necessary to become a married woman before one could have any power to attract a lover. Then, too, what are the poor married folk to do if they don't happen to be like Goethe people, both in love with somebody else? Then the child part of the story, who looks like both the outside lovers, I think rather too peculiar for good taste. But, then, not to admire Goethe is heresy! And to think Shakespeare is a vulgar old—well, I don't know that he was so very old, but he is insufferably vulgar in some of his plays. Look at his '*Measure for Measure*,' for instance; but, then, not to think him an earthly divinity is—oh, my! —almost sacrilege. And, then, the Old Masters!"

"Louisa!" I held up a warning finger. Where was she going to stop?

"Oh! don't stop me, Uncle John, for directly I am going to draw a deduction. After all, novels are not much worse than real life. See how your La Valiéres and Montespans and Pompadours are handed down to posterity, and even your Camilles and Cora Pearls."

"Don't say mine, Louisa," I remonstrated.

"Oh! when I say ' yours,' Uncle John, I am letting you represent the world; but for you, individually, you know I think you a model. But the deduction I was going to make—thinking over all I've read, good, bad and indifferent, translations from popular French works, the chaste opera-bouffe, the lives of most monarchs, and the sweet society divorce drama—was this, that the reading of such things, and it seems to be the bulk of what is popular, tended strongly to make a young girl, or even a married woman, think she must be a little fast, if not worse, to be anybody at all ; and to make the men not only think of following the example set them in books, but to try and far excel their prototypes." I was struck dumb, and as she paused I knew not what to say, for I knew that George's wife was telling—alas! only the truth.

"Well, Uncle John, can't you propose a remedy ?"

"A—hem ! I—I—did you ever read metaphysics, or study botany, or geology, or astronomy, or—"

"Uncle John, Pope says, ' The study of mankind is man,' and that's what I'm studying ; but I should like to discover something to better them—and—yes—I think I would tell it to George."

I smiled quietly, thinking that that same George was the keystone of much of this young lady's homily.

"Uncle John, outside of the great immorality of so much that is written, isn't there a great deal that is ridiculous—the so-called 'funny-men' and some of the dramatic critics ?   I have seen some of them, with their little pasteboard passports from their papers, with their long hair and cadaverous faces, that looked as if they hadn't square meals enough to supply both bodily and mental food ;   and then those ex-pressive-eyed ones, especially when they wear petticoats, how vicious they can be ;   they can sting like a gnat, or an ant, or a flea ;   or if a little jealousy (woman-like) is allowed to influence their judgment, how spiteful they can be ;   then those handsome fellows, who think, like the Pope, that their judgment is infallible, don't they know that they are not the whole public, but only an infinitesimally small part—and not the paying part, either—and that they scarcely represent the opinion of more than their beautiful selves.   They forget that they are *blasé*, having seen the Keans and Macreadys and Forrests, and per-haps the great Siddons ;   but as these people can't come to life again, even for the sake of comparison, and thus this generation has to be contented with the living people of to-day, and that, though they have seen everything, most of the other people have not, and can see beauties in what they have grown too callous to appreciate.   Young blood, Uncle John, is what is needed in the critics of to-day ; not those who have known, seen and enjoyed everything, so are almost worn out and surfeited with the pleasures of this world."

" Louisa !   Louisa !   Where will your tongue lead you ?"

"Uncle John, I've not been out of the house for two weeks, so I'm dying to talk.   The only call I've had was Mrs. Jones, who told me no end of how to make old dresses into new ones, costing more in the end than buying them right out, and as George has not given me any money lately, her visit was not interesting.   Oh !   Uncle John, do come home with me to lunch, I'm so desperately lonely it would be doing a charitable deed."

So I thought, and went.

More anon.

Hop-o'-My-Thumb.

<hr />

ONE MORE UNFORTUNATE.

"Oh! I remember, it is New Year's Day. The last brought many changes. This day twelve-months ! Ah ! Nanine those days are gone —the day that brings new life to every heart."

So said poor Camille, as she lay dying, neglected and alone. Only poor Gaston, at whom she used to laugh, smoothing her pillow, and Nanine the faithful servant, her only friend. Yet for poor, poor Camille's few brilliant years of gilded sin, how many go to a wretched, degraded grave, forgotten before the grass springs above their coffin-lid, thousands following, seeing no lesson in the short, erratic life, the poison or the dark, unpitying water, that opens to them the gates leading to the Shadowy Valley, not heeding the poor girl's dying words:

"It is wise, it is well, it is *just!* I have been guilty ! Living, the memory of that guilt would haunt me like a spectre, darkening, with its fearful shadow, my passage to the close !"

And we wonder and wonder, how can such things be !

Across the street, in a great city, in a fine, clean, quiet-looking house, lived two women, with plenty of servants, elegant clothes, a carriage at their command and nothing to do, but the world said they were *fast*, that their lovers bid them good-bye early in the morning, ashamed for even the daylight to know their hiding-places. Opposite

lived a pretty, ignorant young girl, lazy, slovenly, sometimes almost
lacking food, a mother of whom she was only just a natural copy.
She looked with envy at the elegant females across the street, as they
dashed away in the fine carriage, the stout, respectful negress servant
admiringly waiting to see them off. No word of warning uttered in her
ear, no picture of the white-robed ghost stealing through the narrow,
dimly-lighted streets, to prey upon some wretch, disgusting and re-
pugnant to the lowest semblance of woman, only for her daily bread ;
nothing but the bright side presented to her view, can one wonder that
she falls?

That the one more unfortunate is not multiplied a thousand-fold is
the greatest wonder when one looks beneath the surface of the world's
sufferers. The world's workers are not the ones who fall; it is the
romantic, the lazy, the disappointed, the betrayed. It is not the girl
with the stout heart and courage enough to work for her living, even
if it is at a despised factory, sewing shoes or binding books, or at the
thousand and one occupations now open to women ; it is not the
happy, cherished daughter, whose mind is filled with household duties,
helping mother, or reading well selected books, with a natural love
for the little sisters and brothers—lending them the assistance remembered so well in after years, so needed in their studies and in their
play—with taste cultivated (if only to sing a simple ballad, or sketch in
pencil), whose mind is occupied, leaving no room for foolish vanity,
that too often leads to crime.

It is not the loved wife, whose husband thinks it not unmanly to
love his home, to take the baby on his knee, to relieve his companion
of a little of the care that falls to the lot of the happiest wife and
mother, who is not ashamed to walk with his wife and little ones,
knowing how they enjoy it, even if he does help to draw the little
wagon.

It is not these, whose prayers should rise, morning and night, thanking God for their happiness—it is not these who are picked from the dark waters of the river, or, on the tables of the Morgue, make a pitiful show for the unpitying.

It is the poor, weak girl, with little to do, whose mind is vitiated by bad books, whose home is unhappy, whose idleness gives Satan his best chance ; or the selfish, lazy one, who thinks it better to be well dressed and bad—" others are "—than a drudge and virtuous. It is the disappointed, neglected wife, still young, still pretty, still romantic, who feels so keenly the difference between her home, where she received so much attention, the many friends, the suitors, who were so eager for her smiles ; and the quiet, quiet house, where the ticking of the clock is the only voice to break the stillness far into the night, where she can sob in vain for the presence of the one who vowed to cherish her, but who, too soon, alas, thinks it unmanly to be tied to a woman's apron string ; who goes back to the pastimes of his bachelorhood, forgetful, or not caring that at home is a sorrowful, waiting woman, who endures neglect and loneliness till endurance is a torture and revengeful, bitter feelings makes her a fit prey for the Evil One, and then——. But the husband is pitied and can easily get another victim wife. For her there is no return. Yet God will pity ! God will read her poor heart ; God will know her loneliness, her life unwarmed by sympathy, till wedded love seeming quite a fable, drove her into sin.

For bread, a few sell themselves, till they have sunk to the lowest depths; then the grave is yawning for them grim and horrible.

For love, many die; some with a rash bold hand quickly ending life and pain; others, slowly dying a thousand deaths, pierced as with dagger thrusts by constant pain, cool looks, unkind words, agonies of mind not translatable by words, until faith in man's love is nearly gone.

It is the betrayed, the poor girl who loves too well, and, judging by her own true heart, trusts to vows that are only from the lips. Alas!

alas! poor child, if the pitying waters do not claim thee, call from thy heart for God's great mercy, the streets are apt to be thy home, where, wandering like a restless ghost, sin is met on every side, and Heaven seems so far away; you fear to look upon the stars, lest their pure light remind you of your days of innocence, when you could kiss your mother without a blush, and say "Our Father" with a thankful heart.

It is not too late, dear sisters; God's mercy is for us all; remember the joy in Heaven over the one that repenteth; remember, to suffer is the portion allotted to us all, even the happiest and most fortunate of earth's children; then, do not despair; a little progress every day, a little softening of your heart, a little prayer to God for strength and mercy, and life will look more beautiful and Heaven so near that you will not fear to knock upon the pearly gates, when the last day comes, lest an angry Father drives you hence; but trusting to His tender love, seek Him, as a penitent child, sorrowing, seeks his father's arms.

Dear sisters, let this beautiful, beautiful New Year be a harbinger of hope to your sad hearts; let the next year find you purer, truer in your lives, and in your hearts nearer unto God.

Belle's thoughts.

Hop-O'-My-Thumb.

———

TOO EARLY MARRIAGE.

Almost the first use of the mental development that a girl has attained at school, when she leaves it perfected and accomplished, is to secure a good husband. If she is cold and heartless, it will be done in a mercantile manner, the desirability of the gentleman's worldly position being alone considered ; if she is weak and sentimental, nothing is considered, her ardent fancy changing the most common-place person into a hero. The mind and heart of no girl who has just left school is sufficiently matured to·select a proper companion for life's journey—the union that will secure happiness to both. Marriages of convenience are at the best but shameless bartering of bodies, to the eternal detriment of souls. Hasty, romantic unions should be considered with great caution, for the permanent happiness of one is only the exception to the general rule of misery to the many.

When a girl leaves school she should be allowed and encouraged to see something of the world and mankind. She should be taught that every man who can turn a pretty compliment and wears good clothes is not necessarily the one being of all the world created to bring her happiness. She should be told there are many millions of men in the world, and that the first offer is not of a certainty the last, and that nothing is lost by a reasonable waiting. The father or mother who shows by word or act that they are anxious to get their daughter or their daughters off their hands does not appreciate, and is not faithful to their sacred trust. They should rather be earnest in their endeavors to keep their child in the tender circle of home as long as possible, or at least till a suitor come whom they can reasonably expect to make their daughter happy, for that is the one consideration in marriage above wealth, position, intellect or beauty. The parents should discuss the suitor from every point, sensibly, and even rather leniently, with the girl—not, if they dislike him, showing it in every word, for then she will think they are prejudiced and marry him out of pique and pity—but cooly, critically showing the chances of happiness and misery the wife of such a man would have, and what they would be in such a union as she ought to endeavor to make.

The practice of calling a girl an "old maid" almost before she is out of her teens, is both silly and injurious, causing them sometimes to accept those they would otherwise peremptorily decline, only for fear of those *enfants terrible*, the chipper girls of sixteen, twitting them with old maidism. They should be taught—not all at once, but from their childhood up—that twenty-five is a much more sensible age than the teens in which to take upon themselves the duties and responsibilities of married life, and affords a far better chance for the happiness of all concerned.

How often does the young wife return to her mother's house, sometimes with her little ones, for long visits, to board or to stay till death ! She has left the home-nest too soon; she has made a mistake that perhaps can not be remedied in this world. And the husband should not be ignored, for he is human, the same as the wife, and suffers also, though perhaps not as intensely. A girl in her teens is not physically able properly to endure the care, trials and dignity of motherhood. The sleepless nights, the anxious watching in times of sickness, the unusual confinement from fresh air and sunshine—these tell on her undeveloped constitution, making her prematurely old. She is too young to exercise discretion in the humoring or not humoring the wishes and whims of her husband; too young to understand the benefit of curbing her own temper so as to properly train her husband and children. She is too young to hold the reins of government, even of a small household, with a firm hand, and to preside over it with dignity. Therefore, let her wait till a few years have developed the necessary requisites for her to become a happy wife, and then the suitable husband is easily found.

Mary says this.

HOP-O'-MY-THUMB.

DISAPPOINTMENT.

I am what is impolitely termed an "Old Bach." and, am rather scarce of the capillary growth necessary for an ornament for our kind red brother's wampum belt—in fact, I am a little bald, and that is the reason, I suppose, why the ladies confide in me—making me a repository for their hearts' little secrets.

It was only a few weeks since one young thing came to me and said: "Oh, Uncle John, my heart is broken," and she grasped my hands so tightly that I could not even stroke her shining hair.

"What is the matter, little one?" I asked.

"My husband, my husband—" here she broke down and began to cry.

"The brute!—he has not dared to strike you?"

"Worse than that—a thousand times worse!"

Now I felt my blood rise. Here was a young thing, not eighteen, pretty and not married one short year, and was already crying about her husband's ill-treatment. I bared my arms, and felt as if the strength of Hercules was coming back into the diminished muscles, and that I could fight that man. Then I thought it was well to be prudent in everything, so I said:

"But tell me, little girl, what has he done?"

"Why—why, last night he—he went to see the Living Pictures, and liked them!" and with a burst of grief she threw herself into my arms. How could I console such grief as this? I tried all sorts of commonplaces, but it would not answer.

"You know I thought my husband never looked at another woman,

and—and I was so proud, and bragged to my lady friends, and smiled
in pity when I heard that Mr.——had kissed the hired girl; but she
did have clothes on—at least, I suppose so; but these Living Pictures
haven't got a thing on them, but tights and a bit of gauze. So he told
me with his own lips. Oh, dear! oh, dear!'' and the poor child
rocked herself and moaned, till my eyes were filled with tears, and I
thought what a fool a man was, with a pretty, interesting wife, who
looked up to him as the ideal man of all the world, to kill her faith in
him, to render her suspicious on every occasion of his being at the
" Lodge," for fear he wasn't—all for the sake of seeing a few brazen
women in tights!

" If he had said he wanted to see some living pictures, I would
have been a living picture myself, and the seventy-five cents would
have bought me a new necktie. But I see what it is: he is tired of
me, and wants to see other women. Oh! I wish I had never married!
Could I get a divorce for this?"

I told her I hardly thought she could, although it was provocation
enough. Then, after petting her to quiet her, she arose to go.

" But I'll be revenged. I'll go and flirt with my old beau, Harry; I
wish I had married him!" And she left me to ponder on the disappointments of this life. What age is free from them? From our
earliest infancy, when we fondly imagine the half-pint bottle is inexhaustible, and wake to find we are only imbibing air, the bitter experience begins; it continues as later on we strive to grasp the pretty
flaming candle, and, alas, get only burnt fingers for our pains.

How I could moralize on this! For do not we men—myself ex-
cluded—go after just such dangerous, delusive pleasures and with the
same results? But I am the ladies' confidante. My own sex I ignore
for they have long ago disgusted me. Oh! I could a tale unfold, as
the ghost says, so full of horror, deceit, dreadful wickedness, that my
dear female friends would remain in single-blessedness forever sooner

than trust their happiness in the keeping of that vile creature we call a man. Perhaps you think that disappointment and the world's rough usage has made me a morbid ascetic, seeing things through green spectacles; but I scorn the imputation. My information is gleaned from my dear confidantes, who think me harmless as a wooden image, because my hair is scant and my teeth are out.

It was not long ago, one of the dear creatures met me on the street, and shaking my two hands warmly, said:

"Oh, Uncle John, I'm so glad to see yon. I want your advice. Have you been to lunch?"

On my reply in the negative, she cried:

"Then come along with me, for I am dreadfully hungry!" and she conducted me into a cosy little retreat, where lace curtains shut us out from the vulgar gaze of still hungrier mortals. She ordered a broiled beefsteak, with a coal on it, an omelette, some potatoes (in a delicious style, to me unknown,) and coffee. I said I would take the same, relying on her exquisite taste. And as we ate she talked.

"Oh! Uncle John, I'm so disappointed in my husband."

Ah! this was coming to the point, in a quick, business-like way.

"You don't mean to say so?" I replied, surprised and sympathizing.

"Yes. I've been married—let me see; it seems like six years, but it's only six months Well, George said he didn't drink, chew nor swear. Of course, I didn't mind him smoking those exquisite little cigars he likes. Would you believe it?—two months ago he came home late at night—it was 11 o'clock—and—I do believe he was tight! He said he wasn't; that he didn't feel well, and had taken a little ginger. But it didn't perfume like ginger one bit, and I nearly cried my eyes out. I told him I'd go back to ma's, and he only laughed. Then, I soon discovered he chewed horrid tobacco, like the big, ugly men—and he so handsome! Then, yesterday, because he found a paltry button off his shirt, he said, 'Damn it!' and threw the shirt on the floor."

She looked as if she would cry, but she did not stop eating. I was glad of it, for she needed all the strength to be got from nutritious food to bear up under such brutality.

"Well, my dear," I began, "you should not have married a man with the idea he was an angel! Did none of your experienced lady friends inform you that men were not altogether to be relied on, and that their habits were not quite as refined as a young girl's?"

" But, Uncle John, George was so sweet; why half the girls I knew were in love with him. He had the dearest little moustache—and to think that it should be stained with that horrid—but that isn't all; he he has joined the Lodge, and the Sons of something, and always has so much business with them that I hardly have his company one evening a week. When I was single he wanted to come twice a day, but ma wouldn't let him. Why I should be so much less attractive because I happen to marry him, I can't see, for if I had taken Ned— I almost wished I had—he said he would blow his brains out, and that he would never cease to love me. According to this, it is better to marry a man you don't care for, so that the one you do love shall always care for you. "

" Why, you are quite a little philosopher! Yes, I have heard that men care sometimes more for some one else's wife than they do for their own. But in your case, I shouldn't think that possible. Indulge him a little; don't let him see tears. Men like them well enough in a lady-love, but in a wife—well, they drive the husband out of doors, and then you don't know what he does. Be cheerful; give him a cuspador in each room; and if he will drink Boca, get a pitcher of it for dinner and drink it with him. Ask him if you can join the Lady Grangers, or the Sorosis, or something exclusively feminine; tell him if he can't take you, Ned will be only too happy to do so. Work a little on his jealousy; not too much; just keep up his interest in you. Let him see you are not unattractive to all others, and always look pretty, and good tempered, and I think he won't be such a fool as to neglect the good he has for unknown and dangerous attraction."

The young puss smiled.

" I did think of seeing about a divorce, but I guess I'll try George a few months more. Oh, Uncle John, if the men were all like you! But you are an angel!"

And this poor child is only one of millions like her.

HOP-O' MY-THUMB.

This is George's wife's secret.

WOMAN---PAST, PRESENT AND FUTURE.

I stand up in defence of my sex. I stand up to hurl the gauntlet of defiance into the face of that old octogenarian, the London *Saturday Review*.

I stand up to defy the writers, young and old, rich and poor, male or female, who wilfully and with malice-aforethought, villify the Present Woman.

Even my friend, the magnificent *Alta*—stop, let me think; no, it was the not so magnificent Saturday's *Post*—gave a column and a half of back-handed slaps, at our devoted sex.

All these writers whine regretfully over what the sex was, deprecate what it is, and look with fearful foreboding to what it will be.

The blushing, drooping modesty of a century ago was well enough for feudal days and feudal castles, when the faintest shriek from fair lips would summon a dozen knights errant and cavaliers to the distressed one's side; when a woman was only expected to look pretty and work embroidery; when mead ran in the cellar, and whole carcasses of beef hung in the pantry; when nothing more serious than the Troubadour's latest song occupied the fair one's mind; then, indeed, the blushing, drooping modesty that the octogenarian, the *Post*, and the little fish bewail, was the fitting and expected characteristic of the sex that then dared hardly raise their eyes to the faces of their lords.

But in this rushing, bustling world, a woman is considered as good as another man, to fight the battle of life, but not to have quite as good a right.

Why, I've seen a little woman just out of a sick bed, and not tall enough to reach the strap, stand during a long ride in a street car; she had as much right to stand as a healthy man, and she did. Her blushing, or rather pale modesty didn't help her much. I've seen these delicate creatures—whom the writers of the day deplore as having lost the blushing aforesaid—nearly pushed into the gutter, to make way for a strong man; they had just as good a right to get their dainty feet muddy as he; in fact I've felt the hard elbows in my own side, and never even pushed back in retaliation, but I've ground my teeth, and thought naughty things.

It's all very pretty to read about this drooping modesty, and occasionally would light up well as a picture, with damask and lace curtains as a background, and a hanging lamp and handsome young man as auxiliaries, but for practical use in this work-a-day world, we want just such women as we have got—hard-headed and hard-handed, too, sometimes, with a dogged determination to hold their own, even against a thousand male competitors.

I will tell you some facts to support my arguments. In Philadelphia in the year 187–, there were two lady engravers, and but two who made it a profession, so I was told, in the whole city. One of them

I knew; she worked for years, illustrating *Godey's Lady's Book*, and her work was as good as that in any cotemporary magazine; but the male engravers—I will not call them men—determined that those two women should not be competitors even if they had to do the work for that magazine for nothing; so they underbid and underbid them, till at last they got their wish, and years of faithful service was forgotten in that goodly city, because the stronger sex wanted no women rivals, so would work cheaper—at least till they got rid of them.

Then again, one of these ladies was for years the teacher of engraving in a School of Design. A man came and offered to teach for nothing; magnanimous creature! and the female—shaming her sex— who conducted the establishment, accepted the offer. How long he taught for nothing after this gallant action is not hard to surmise.

Will the London *Saturday Review*, and the thousand and one other howlers, please tell us what retiring, modest simplicity would have accomplished in these cases? Perhaps a deluge of tears, or a few fainting fits would have softened these male creatures' hearts, and the weak sisters would have been permitted to earn their own living in peace ; but we doubt it. And such are the people and circumstances women have daily to encounter in this weary struggle for existence Is it not enough to rub the blush and bloom off beauty's cheek, to harden the native delicacy of her feelings, to make her try to educate herself as man to meet man ?

This is all very well, you may think, for the working class; but this is a great class. Watch the streets of a large city at 6 P. M., near the manufactories, and you will be surprised to see the crowds of girls and women, with their little baskets and bundles ; then there are thousands who do not go in crowds, from the photograph galleries, the counters, the school rooms, the theatres, the printing offices, the opera singers, the servant girls, and our poor, poor, despised saloon waiters and singers.

One-half of this vast army has been as delicately brought up as the blushing-modesty people could wish, but they soon find that actual life is somewhat different from romance, and that the Don Quixotes are, alas! all dead ; that the prizes are for those that can battle the hardest, and not for the retiring, easily vanquished woman.   Is it a wonder, then, that their air is a little more defiant than may be desirable, or their voice a shade louder, or their lives more independent ?

I despise the girl or woman who is always looking out for an insult, and can make a double *entendre* of every little joke that's uttered.   I've seen such ; these are the horse-whipping, cow-hiding kind.   I've seen that, too, in one of the largest eastern theatres, where the women screamed, " Don't let him hit her," when the " he" apparently had no intention of doing anything but holding the infuriated woman's arms. I thought her blushing-modesty deserved a right smart beating in return.

I've heard of the blushing kind replying to the remarks of strangers and then when one shows pretty plainly what he thinks she is, she is indignant and calls on her big brother, or avenges her own honor in some public place.   Had she walked on, with her eyes before her, attending to her own affairs, in a sensible, business-like way, not trying the game of drooping eyelids and faltering footsteps, to be admired as so unsophisticated ! she could go through the world without one insult, or many occasions to do blushing either.

We want to know where the women of to-day have so deteriorated that all these cries should be raised against them; can't they do as much as they ever did? Aye, a thousand times more! Look how many women support their families, or help their husbands to do so, or provide for a mother, or dependent little sisters and brothers! in so many different branches of industry, too, that a few years ago were sealed books to women.

Letters from the great Exposition tells of some good inventions emanating from female brains. One, a fire-proof building material, which if it be all that is claimed, will prove a valuable epoch in the world's history. In our own little fair here, women made their presence known with their sweet tar drops, and their hair restorer; and who will deny the palm to a woman for the boon of all boons—at least most married men think so—Mrs. Winslow's Soothing Syrup? How many a night would the masculine rest be broken, the peaceful dreams annihilated, the morning nap disturbed, had not kind Providence permitted the woman Winslow to be born and bred.

Education, too, is more universal than it ever was before; and as for the modesty in dress, no one who looks at a lady's magazine of fifty or sixty years ago, will pretend that our dear ancestors set us an example that could be followed without the greatest scandal in these—according to their cry—degraded days. A petticoat or gown of the scantiest pattern, showing foot, ankle, shape and bosom; a net work of pearls or gold braid covering the whole, until the extravagance was prohibited by a decree from the throne. I've seen the book—tiny slippers, long white gloves, a few short fleecy curls, and a lady was in full dress for court or ball.

And they cry, too, so much about a woman's make up; this is of nonsense the very sheerest. In the car the other day, of all the women there, some eight or more, I could almost take my—I was going to swear! oh, my!—that not one was the least made up by pad or bustle, hair or jute, paint or powder, except the little that perhaps remained on my face, and that the great majority of women are likewise as nature made them.

Those that are made up, what does it amount to? A little cotton where nature has been illiberal, a newspaper to give the dress a proper set, and a little powder to soften the effect of tan or freckles. There are a few exceptions to the rule, of course, but not enough to warrant the conclusion that we are all going headlong to the—.

These very croakers would smile sweeter, and raise their hats higher to a pretty woman, even if they knew that art helped to make her a joy forever, than they would to a rusty, dusty simplicity, with a drooping head and a giggle.

I can imagine drooping, blushing modesty changed into a wife of to-day; after the first three weeks her husband would tell her she was a fool to be so sensitive, and not to blush whenever a person looked at her, as if she was ashamed of herself; and ten to one she would have to gird up her loins for a good day's washing before many months were over, if she hadn't the spirit to say "I shan't!" and stick to it.

I don't depreciate modesty, mind me, but maintain that the women of the present day are as modest as is necessary to good sense—in fact as modest as they ever were.

Helen's opinion.

A PLEA FOR LAZINESS.

Laziness, all hail! thou fat, innocent goddess, to whom people give no credit of good performed of any kind; let me defend thee, not as an advocate, only to show thy uses and abuses in a clear, dispassionate way.

Let us begin at the beginning.

The baby in its innocent infancy is by no manner of means a lazy atom of humanity; yet what does it accomplish? If its perpetual force of lung and limb could be put to some purpose, the motive power of many a mill and factory could be had without steam—a thought—could it not be utilized to grind the matutinal coffee, or to turn a handle, and polish the paternal boot? But I digress.

Who does not shrink from the stinging remark: "This is a lazy thing!" Yet who is it that becomes fat and fair at forty? Why, the lazy female, to be sure, who sits at the window with folded hands, and watches the moving crowds in the streets, who goes to bed early and has a good, long, morning nap.

People often call it a clear conscience when one can nap, morning, noon and night, but the real name is laziness, pleasant to the practicer, but sometimes very selfish, and inconvenient to others.

It's nice to have a clear conscience, and sleep so sound that the baby's screams don't wake you, nor the nudges of your wife disturb you; it's nicer to be so innocent that you, in your dreams, are soaring with the angels, while your better half, in night robe and bare feet, is walking the floor with your son and heir or warming his "pap" over the gaslight.

It's nice to be able to call selfishness and laziness by pretty, meritorious names, thus satisfying one's conscience.

It's nice to have such an innocent, child-like disposition that you can sleep all Sunday afternoon, when your wife would so enjoy a walk with you. It saves you the annoyance of her silly prattle and the absurdity of being seen with a baby in your arms. It's nice to go to bed at eight o'clock so as not to be bored visiting your wife's relations, or spending your money for two at shows when it is so much nicer to play "Pedro nine" at the corner for cigars or—don't mention it— drinks; and as you cannot sleep forever, its pleasant and independent, and not lazy, to get up at 4 A. M. and wander in and out, slamming the doors when others want to sleep; but you're not a lazy slug-a-bed, and they ought not to be either.

But to our lean, long, restless sisters, we would recommend a little of this clear conscience, sometimes called "laziness." They work too much; take the average farmer's wife for example, brown, careworn and angular, looking years older—though she is not—than her fat rosy husband; watch her day's occupations: a candle-light breakfast in Winter, to prepare which, Heaven knows at what hour she got up;

milking, dish-washing, house-cleaning, churning, washing, ironing, mending, bread-baking, cooking; in Summer, canning, preserving and pickling added, varied a little by spinning yarn or making her husband's jeans; in addition to these amusements, a half dozen to a dozen shock-headed likenesses of their father to attend to. No time to cultivate the intellect, or taste, or even a flower garden; a weekly or monthly paper to snatch a glimpse of on Sunday, when their lord is sleeping; a pinch of the chin, or a kiss, an unknown and almost forgotten recompense for a harder, more wearying day's work than a man can ever know. These are the women who work themselves into early graves, and for whom their husbands mourn for just one month and a half, and at the end of the second month, clean shaven and shod, and dressed in a suit of new store-clothes, begin to go to meetin' regularly and watch the girls and widows, seein' one home when the least chance is offered.

It is not only our country sisters who need the prescription "a little laziness, taken after meals," but many of the bustling wives of the city, who do all their own work, and their husbands smoke two-bit cigars.

This is the Work.

Oh, take advice from one who knows. Don't work yourselves to death. No one will care one jot the more for you; your husband won't love you any better; in fact, I think a little contrary - wise; your hard hands, and your wrinkled brows will only make him say, or think, you are growing old and ugly—then—

Laziness all hail!

And perhaps you think no great inventions have emanated from the brains of lazy people, or rather from their exigencies. I have been told by various people, but do not affirm of my own knowledge, for I mightn't even have been born at the time, for aught I know, of two valuable additions to the inventions of science, caused by laziness, or rather, laziness being the motive-power—one, the steam gauge.

A boy, being left to watch the engine, had to get up at certain intervals and let off the steam, and he was one of the kind who didn't like to get up at certain or uncertain intervals, so he made a contrivance of string and wire, and old iron, to let the steam off for him, while he remained on his stool to read or doze, and this was the basis of the valuable steam gauge.

The next, the fireproof material for safes. An Italian plaster image-maker used to wash his hands in cold weather in a basin of water that constantly stood on the stove. He was not one of those who liked clean water so well that he would take the trouble to change it each time he washed the plaster from his hands; so there it staid till it would no longer become hot, even with a good fire beneath it. And this is how the non-conducting of heat quality was discovered, both of plaster of Paris and certain cements, an invention ensuing which, we all know, has saved much valuable property.

Then the old chap who so lazily watched the kettle, and thus discovered the power of steam. See how his laziness has revolutionized the world!

Franklin, too, flying his little kite (for indulging in which sport many a boy has got a licking for laziness). See what he discovered—touching off the electricity of the clouds.

And Newton, too. His lazy lounging under a tree, watching the apples fall, discovered to us the reason why we don't fly off this globe on a tangent when we are upside down, as it were.

Has Laziness nothing to boast of in these illustrious examples, I should like to know?

If the truth was known, no doubt but many, very many, of our labor-saving inventions could be traced to the quality inherent in many people, of trying to condense their work, or to perform it with as little trouble and expense of strength as possible.

Look at the dumb-waiter; who would have thought of that but the person who did not like to give their calves too much exercise; the elevator, ditto; the rolling chair at the great centennial, ditto, ditto.

And the washing fluids, and the labor-saving soaps, that you are only to cut up and put in the water with the clothes, look at them hard, turn them over once, and they're done. Could any but a lazy person have thought of a way to get a boiled shirt so easily?

Look at the reapers and mowers, the threshers and crushers of the present day—do the horses eat more hay because it is cut easier? Do the cows consume more fodder, or the tippler more corn juice, or the farmer live longer, because of these inventions? No. But Laziness said: " If we have them we'll have more time for play ;" and where there is a demand, there always is a supply. So all hail to Laziness! for it gives the farmer more time to read and cultivate his intellect and become a Granger ; and though they don't take but little work from the woman, save in the fearful large dinners they used to have to get up for the harvesters, yet she, too, becomes inoculated with progress, and, following in the footsteps of her husband, becomes a Grangeress.

Now, mind me, I like a clean house, although I don't like to make it so myself ; and I don't like my servant to neglect to dust the mantles and furniture, and keep a good look out for the damage the flies do. I don't like slippery dishes, either, and murky glasses, or sooty tins, or greasy floors ; yet, when dire necessity compels my ninety-two pounds avoirdupoise to not only superintend and manage, but also to practice, I am dainty with my fingers, not wishing to burn them ; I can't or do not like to stoop, so the floors get scrubbed ———. Then I am conveniently near-sighted, and when my beloved blanks the cobwebs, I say :

" Where dear ?   I can't see them."

And you know it would be a cruel man that could blame his wife's infirmity of sight, so he takes the broom and brushes them down, swallowing his wrath with a grunt !

" Umph !"

This is what Emily thinks.

SMALL FEET.

Why is it that gentlemen so admire small feet ? If a little foot is good, a large one ought to be better. That stands to reason; but I am not so young as I was, and perhaps look at these things in a more philosophical light. We pretend to admire striped stockings; then, of course, the more stripes visible the greater our admiration; *ergo*, the larger the foot, the more stripes.

The weaker sex dress to please us lords of creation, so 'tis said, reiterated, and said again; so then to us belongs the blame of inciting a damsel with a No. 5 foot to wear a No. 2½ shoe. Think of the pains and aches we are responsible for; think of the corns and bunions our opinions have planted! Observe the hesitating, uneven steps! we know the poor thing is in misery, and all for what ? To show a smaller shoe than she can comfortably wear, because we admire them.   But as we do not feel the pain, I suppose we should not complain, especially those of us who dote on small feet, and do a little suffering in that way ourselves.

Why, I know a young man who has as small a foot as a lady; but mind me, I don't say he suffers for it; perhaps it is a natural gift, not an acquired one.   I know another who can wear his wife's shoes, and it don't make him proud one bit; oh, no! we stern sex are never proud, not even over our physical beauties, over which the ladies go in raptures. Why I've heard them myself, exclaim: "Oh! what an exquisite little foot he has!" And if the possessor thereof had heard himself, do you suppose a blush of pleasurable vanity would have suffused his cheek? Oh, no! when a man has a small foot he knows it well, if not by the aches aud pains of tight boots, then by the oft-repeated remarks and admiring glances of the fair sex.

Observing human nature as I do, I have come to the conclusion, if the sexes could change places, what attentive, devoted lovers the weaker sex would be !

Apropos of small feet, I was riding in a street car the other day— not one of those popular ones, the seats of which are so old and wretched that ladies have to cover them with newspapers to keep from soiling their dresses, but one of those nice, clean wooden-seated ones —when a lovely damsel of sweet sixteen entered. Her dress was of the most approved style, flounced and puffed and pulled back. Balancing herself on the edge of the seat, she pulled on her gloves ; they fitted like her own fair skin;   then she deliberately, and without

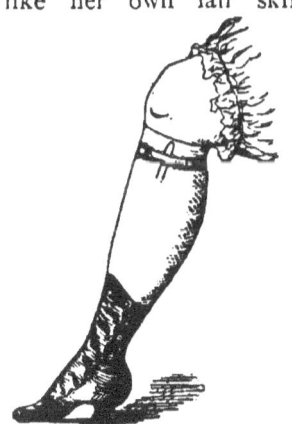

giving previous notice, so that modest men could leave the car, she deliberately *raised her dress and pulled from her garter* a large hair-pin, buttoned the aforesaid gloves, replaced the popular buttonhook, smoothed down her dress, and sat smiling ! * We gentlemen stood aghast. Mr. I——, a young man of my acquaintance studying for the ministry had fainted, in the corner. Mr. V——, a stockbroker, had frantically grasped the bell-strap and without waiting for the car to stop, nearly landed in the cold waters of the Fountain. I covered my face with my handkerchief and wept, almost; yet she sat smiling, cool and possessed.

This is the leg.

*This really occurred, a ew days ago, in a street car in the city of San Francisco

That young female could rule a kingdom ; could order a man's head cut off without any emotion ; could command armies, burn the Sioux in their own fires, and wear the scalp of Sitting Bull !

Oh, but her foot !—my handkerchief was thin—her dear, exquisite foot ! so small, so shapely, so perfectly encased in the fitting kid ! Then her stockings !—never, should I die for it, could I tell you their color ; but they clung to her perfect limbs with such loving closeness that they seemed to have grown there—and I groaned there, too.

Hop o'-my-Thumb.

Peter told this to his wife, who told it to me.

WHY DO MEN MARRY.

I was sitting in my office—did I tell you that I had an office ? Well, it was on the first floor, the last of a long series of rooms ; the passage is not very light, nor clean, still the sun streams into my room at certain hours of the day, lights up my desk and dingy books and the square of faded carpet, so it doesn't look so very bad, and I'm rarely without a little nosegay from some one of my confidential female friends ; this gives the bit of color for the picture. I'm not exactly a lawyer, or a broker, or a poet, but I combine the three in a sort of a way, and with the addition of advisor, I manage to make my living. 'Tis true, I'm not extravagant, and a laudatory poem oftens gets me a pair of new breeches, or a coat or a vest, they don't always match, but still I'm very presentable to lunch with my fair friends.

Well, I was sitting in my office ruminating on human nature in general, and the sorrows of the gentler sex in particular, when a timid rap sounded on the partially open door—I always keep my door open, not wishing any "ragged-edge" scandal about me.

"Come in," I cried in a business-like voice, and George's wife—I won't tell her name, for fear you would recognize her—came in, her pretty face looking like an April sky. After the usual salutations were over, and I had ensconced her in my great comfortable leathern chair she burst out :

"Oh ! Uncle John, what do the men marry for ?"

The question surprised, nay, I must confess, rather staggered me, and I am generally equal to any emergency, but in a moment I answer.

"Why, to have the constant companionship, the endearments, the moral support of just such charming little angels as you."

"That's what I thought six months ago ; but experience is a bad teacher !"

"What ! young, handsome, six months married, and—"

"It's more than six months, Uncle John—it's six months and two weeks."

"And do you begin to find experience such a hard teacher ?"

"Uncle John," she said, solemnly and mysteriously, "I wouldn't have believed it— no one, not even an angel, could have made me believe six months ago that the nice little dinners I get up would have to be kept in the oven till the dishes crack, and the plates get so hot that George swears—would you believe it ?—*swears* at burning his fingers handling them, when he has kept them there for one or two hours waiting for him ! Who could be a good housekeeper if their husband has no regular hours for his meals?"

"I thought he liked a good dinner ?"

"So he does ! that's why I cannot understand why he will stop at the corner to finish a rubber of whist, when he knows that the dinner is ready, and that the steak is the very best in the market ; and, as he is an amateur cook, he knows while he is finishing that hateful rubber, the steak loses the fine flavor it has on just leaving the fire—it makes me so mad. I'd almost as leave have no dinner."

What could I suggest to ameliorate this sad condition of affairs? Ah—

"My dear, why don't you leave the cooking of the steak till he comes?

"Oh! I've tried that; then he says; 'Darn it! I thought dinner was ready.' Then, when I try to explain how I wished him to have it just from the fire, the fire that was so bright half an hour ago, it is either nearly out, or filled with fresh coal, then he gets mad. Oh, dear!" and she sighed, "I didn't dream all a married woman has to endure! This is only one item; I should tire you if I told you all."

"Well, my dear, you will settle down after a while, and become accustomed to each other's ways."

"Oh! Heaven forbid I should ever become accustomed to the cold dinners, or the dried-up dinners, or wasting half my time waiting; and as to settling down, why he never has time (?) to take me any place now, and to all intents and purposes I may as well be old and ugly, and a little crippled, into the bargain."

" My dear, do you make your home comfortable and pretty; have you pictures, statuettes, books, and nicknacks lying around?" Here she fairly burst out laughing.

"Oh, Uncle John, Uncle John; you dear old unsophisticated angel." And she threw her arms about my neck, and, yes—I could not be mistaken— absolutely kissed me on the cheek. Was she losing her reason, with all her troubles?

"Why, Uncle John, don't you know that George don't care a—— for pictures, statues and things; so has furnished the parlor very neatly with plain carpet and a set of furniture; dining-room ditto, without a carpet? But as I like the little trifles that make home pleasant, especially as it is the one place I see and live in, nine-tenths—yes, more than that— of the time, I want something beside bare walls to look at; do you know what I do?"

"Why, buy those things that you admire with the pocket-money your husband gives you." Here came another fit of laughing ; so I moved my chair a little, being rather nervous.

"Why—I'll call you a goose, this time.   Does a man ever give his wife pocket money? None of my friends have any—unless they ask a good many times for it ; and I'll beg no man—not even if I am married to him—for a little paltry money ; so I just go through his pockets when he is asleep—to see if they need mending, of course—and then, as I'm supposed to be his other half, I divide the contents. So I've—why, Uncle John, why do you look so horrified?"

I was aghast.   This was the first time in all my confidences that any lady had boldly acknowledged to going through her husband's pockets! Perhaps, after all, I had done wisely in not marrying.

"But, my child," I presently managed to say, "is not that rather—" "Not at all, Uncle John ; why all we married ladies do it ; or where would our matinee money come from, or our lunch down town, or our gloves, or any little luxury?

This is the divide.

Why, George thinks as long as I've a dress, petticoat and shoes on I'm dressed; and as I wear his soiled collars turned, he never knows but I have an inexhaustible supply.   But as other gentlemen often see me in the garden or on the street, I have to dress for them and my lady friends."

"All married men are not the same, surely?"

"I don't know, but from what my friends say it's pretty much six of one and half a dozen of the other.   But I was going to tell you how I try to beautify my home on little or nothing. I've bought a dollar table. Oh, those dollar stores are invaluable for taste and poverty.

So I keep a fresh bouquet, cut from our little garden, always on it; that livens the room up a bit. Then I've bought a dollar mat, with a dog on it. George likes dogs, so I thought it would please him. Then I made coffee berry frames for the three graces that came with a weekly, and two pretty twenty-five cent chromos; and you have no idea how much more home-like the room looks. Oh! I forgot the fly trap made of white muslin, that I hung on the gas burner—you see we don't use gas, it's too dear—and the box I covered with red and black flannel for a footstool; and the books, I thought he should not complain of lack of intellectual food, so last week I bought 'Daniel Deronda' and *Harper's Weekly*. But it don't keep him in the house any more—all these embellishments—for he reads 'Daniel' when he wakes in the middle of the night and smokes his cigar, and the pictures in *Harper's* occupied him just five minutes."

All my well-known phrases of consolation and advice would not touch this case; so, after rubbing my nose thoughtfully, I could only say:

"Let us hope for the best."

"Yes, but Uncle John, why do men want to marry, try so hard to win us, yes, and, I must say it, tell so many lies, too, about how devoted they'll be? They could live on a desert island forever if we alone were there, and that we are the only woman in the world for them? Oh! they all say the same, for my friends told me so. Why don't they speak the truth right out, and say they want to marry us to look after their buttons, see their shirts are not stolen by the China washerman, that their dinner is ready whenever they want it, and to have somebody when it's cold to warm their beds?"

" My dear!"

" Oh! it's true, Uncle John! and I love my husband dearly, and I wouldn't change him now for any man I know; but if love is blind, I don't believe it, for I love and yet see his many faults; but never mind,

I'm hungry, so let's go to lunch; I've only got two dimes and a car ticket—I guess George was broke last night—but I know a place in the market right near, where we can get shrimps, bread and butter, and the nicest cup of coffee you ever tasted for ten cents each—let's go."

So I put on my hat and went.

HOP-O'-MY-THUMB.

Louisa's Secret.

DANIEL DERONDA---VOLUME SECOND.

I did not untie the pink wrapping string of volume the second, with eager haste, in a dimly lighted car, as I did that of No. 1. I knew what I expected, and was so little moved by any powerful emotion, that I had allowed more than a month to pass, before this volume rested in my hand.

As I read, I wondered what could be the secret of Daniel's popularity, or rather why had the work brought so much money to the author, for that the book is popular—meaning by that, liked by the mass of readers, I do not believe.

In an interval of my second day's reading of the last volume, happening to meet an acquaintance, and speaking of what I was doing, he remarked :

'' Daniel was a little disappointing, was'nt he ?"

I could only truthfully acquiesce. Then meeting George's wife shortly after, on her way to invest in stocks, she exclaimed:

" Oh! Uncle John, I didn't like that old book you lent me, one bit; a couple of my friends have read it, and they don't like it at all, either!"

" But, my dear, don't you admire the subtle philosophizing, that the critics so commend ?"

"Subtle bosh! If I wanted to read a treatise on the Jews, I would have bought one, and I should hope it would be a little less obscure, and tell a little more what it meant, than Mordecai's ravings."

"My dear, you are not yet educated up to it, that's plainly to be seen."

"And I don't want to be either; when a person's philosophizing is so very deep, that each page of the same requires an hour's study to get even a faint glimmering of the meaning, it's about time to class novels with metaphysics, and study them at school. How do you like Gwendolen, for instance?"

"She is a very sweet woman, or has the making of one, rightly circumstanced, and her husband is a heartless brute!"

"Ha! ha! ha! Ho! ho! ho! Uncle John, that's just like you men; you take the part of any woman, no matter how mean or bad she is, *provided she is not your own wife.*"

"And ain't it just the reverse with you ladies, my dear? You go against every female no matter how good she is, just because she is a female."

"Indeed, you are mistaken; but what would you think of me, if I carried a sharp dagger about me, and thought continually how I could use it, where it would do most good—excuse my slang, nunckey— just because George objected to my flirting with Ned, or wanting to see him alone every day in the week, to tell him how very naughty I was, for coming between my husband and an old sweetheart, and how very, very disappointed I was, because I could not hold my lord under my thumb."

"But, Louisa,"—this was the first time I had ever called her by her Christian name, and my temerity almost startled me—"See how meanly he began to treat her from their very wedding day."

"Meanly! why if George paid me as much attention as he did her, I should feel myself in the seventh Heaven! He did not differ a bit

from what he was as a lover, except he felt well enough acquainted to
d— things occasionally; and I should like to see the husband who
does not, sooner or later, use that privilege.   I heard of one the other
night, but he isn't dead yet!"

" I'm afraid you are not a deep student of human nature."

" Do you mean by that, that it is only human and womanly for
every lady who is compelled by a stronger will than her own, to yield
an unwilling obedience, to wish the person dead, if it happens to be
her husband, and to have very little compunctions about helping him
to that state, either ?"

"Oh! no! I didn't mean that!"

"Divest her of her statuesque form, her serpentine neck, and her
narrow eyes, let her be Mrs. Flannigan, subdued to obedience, not by
a strong will and a steady glance, but by a strong hand and a black
eye, or by what many of Gwendolen's less fortunate sisters have often
received, a good hiding, in the language of the British lords, and you
wouldn't feel so sentimental about her."

"Do men ever beat their wives?"

"Why you unsophisticated thing! Do you never read the newspapers ?"

"Yes. But I thought those Bohemian inventions as jokes on the sex!"

"I guess some of the sex wish they were.   But about Gwendolen,
to whom the author devotes so many pages, trying to make clear to
the readers, her true inwardness, and yet lets her turn out to be less
than nothing—but I suppose that gives a good chance for a sequel; but
don't you think her a murderess in her heart, and with less excuse than
millions of her sex have, this very day and hour ?"

" I can hardly think that."

"Umph! If you were a married man I could convince you. Suppose you had lots of money."

" I wish I had"—*sotto voce.*

"And had married a poor but rather pretty girl, given her mother a good income, and loaded her with jewels and fine dresses; that you were tolerably young and good looking—"

"I was, a few years ago."

"Took her to balls, parties, journeys, and thought enough of her to feel jealous, wouldn't you think if she wasn't happy she must have a bad heart and a very discontented mind? And if she consented so gladly to your being drowned, not trying to help save you, when it was in her power, till too late, you'd think it but a lame excuse, that he ordered her how to work the tiller, and persuaded her unwillingly to go boating—I only wish George would take me boating!—when she wanted to have a flirtation, or to confess for the twentieth time, how naughty she was to a dear friend, wouldn't you think her a fit subject for a trial and the penitentiary, instead of ten thousand a year and a fine house ?"

" ' Now you put it in that light, I don't think I would like to be her second husband. But Mirah and Deronda—there are some very good characters in the book."

" It would be a pity if there was'nt, and the author receive, as is said, about thirty thousand dollars for her work. Didn't you recognize a great similarity between Deronda and Julian Grey, especially in the chapter where Gwendolen steals away from the walking party, and hurries back, to catch Daniel in the library ? It's so much like a scene from the New Magdalen."

" Yes, I noticed that several of their interviews bore evidence that the author had been impressed with Wilkie Collins' work; also that in the employment of Lush, to communicate the contents of the will, there was something strongly suggestive of Dombey and Son; but I suppose it's true 'there's nothing new under the sun.' "

" It's truer that ' nothing is so successful as success ;' and when people read of how into the hundred thousands the receipts of Daniel

went, every one wanted a copy, thinking it must be something wonderful.   Now the subtle philosophizing that seems to be so spoken of,
I consider the utterings of a dreamer, who sees things but visionary,
and tries by a multitude of words, to express images which are but em-
bryos of thoughts in the writer's mind."

" Whew ! Why, Louisa, that's the most learned sentence I ever
heard you speak !"

" Oh, indeed! because I'm good tempered, lively, and little, I suppose you thought I had no sense."

" No, my dear; but women seem to be so taken up with dress, and
petty gossip, that—"

" Oh! Uncle John, don't slander our sex!   You know we have to
dress, and we have to talk, yet we still have time to cultivate our
brains a bit, and have some little opinion of our own about the books
we read, and I must say that Daniel Deronda made me have the blues,
and be melancholy and cross for two days, especially during the time
I read his interviews with his mother; such a hard hearted woman as I
believe, never lived in heaven or on earth."

"What! do you think singers or actresses have the same feelings as
other women ?"

"Why shouldn't they ? and be even more intense in their loves and
hates, as they must understand every passion in order to depict them
with any degree of satisfaction to an intelligent audience.   It is a
back-handed slap to a great profession, that is very unkind and gratu-
itous of George Elliot.   But, there. I've talked till I'm hungry; come
across the street with me till I see about some 'Dardinelles;' it'll be
worth ever so much some day, then you shall come to my house and
take lunch.   I've got some real nice crab salad that George caught in
the bay—not the salad, but the crabs—plenty of mustard in it, and
I'll make you a nice cup of tea."

I sighed as I shook my head, remembering I had no car tickets, and
no portion of the Comstock Lode in my pocket to buy any, so I went
home and read the advertisements in the back of "Daniel Deronda,"
which I'll sell now for half price, or a dozen street-car tickets. Adieu.

HOP-O'-MY-THUMB.

COURTING.

I was shocked, horrified, almost dumbfounded! There was Miss Sarah (she calls herself Sallie) in the parlor with her two beaux, and and her father, mother and sister, in the kitchen with the pots and pans, to which latter place I was invited to enter. I did so, sitting on the edge of a chair, and sharing with the others in an impatient waiting for the young men to finish their remarks about the weather, and their critical analysis of the various performances of Edwin Booth; but their departure hung fire; perhaps each tried to sit the other out, or the society of the charming Sarah might have been too fascinating to have been easily dispensed with. At all events, I left while their forced laughs of merriment were still stealing through cracks and keyholes. I went home and ruminated.

These are the beaux.

When I was young, and my sisters—I had four of them—had company, no one thought of leaving the parlor while the favored young gents aired their ideas of matters and things in general. Gracious ! it would have taken four parlors to have accommodated each separate sister if their courting was to be as mysterious and secret as the holding of a Freemason's Lodge! But girls in those days were different; they honored their parents, and thought it was quite as well to find out their lover's characteristics in the bosom of their families, where papa could joke them, and the little ones could pull their hair, and demand contributions of candy, and where a kiss at the gate, and sundry stolen glances in the parlor was considered a good night's courting, and a blissful reward for a five miles walk. But they have changed, and marriages are not so numerous, and no wonder, for when a young girl banishes the family from the parlor, she deliberately says in actions, which, they say, speak louder than words:

"My dear Charles Augustus, here I am alone; now court me. I expect to entrap you for a husband, and the folks are so eager to get rid of me, that they will give us the exclusive use of the parlor, so that I can have every possible chance to exercise the power of my charms, for an indefinite number of weeks to accomplish that wished for result."

Now, is it strange that breach of promise cases are numerous, when a man is almost forced to propose, and then so deluged with sweetness before the wedding day, that he is surfeited and thinks he has made a mistake ; that there is so little left to find out about the young lady that all the novelty is gone; that he could not be happy with her; in fact, he gets to rather dislike her. And so Clorinda weeps over broken vows, or if she is of a practical turn of mind, estimates her sorrows at so many thousands of dollars, and confides her heart's secrets to the tender confidence of a sensational lawyer.

" Umph! you'd like a girl to marry a man who had never been permitted to gaze upon her lovely face, like in those wicked old Eastern countries," some of my sweet friends might say. But no, I would have a happy medium, where kisses and caresses were not so numerous as to be no novelty after marriage. I would leave a little to the imaignation and to the anticipation. I would have it so, that if the acquaintance developed characteristics that were disagreeable either could retreat without having the whole community scandalized, and the edge of the lady's purity so dulled that a second suitor would be loth to present himself.

All night long I dreamed of courting, lovers' quarrels, breaches of promise, weeping maidens, sarcastic young men; a very kaleidoscope of the affections, and I arose at the first break of day, and deluging my face and head in cold water, soon dispelled the illusions of the night.

As the day wore on, George's wife rapped at my office door.

" My dear, you're just the person I wanted to see." Then I asked her ideas on the subject of the exclusiveness of courting. She burst out into a merry laugh and said :

" I want no big, glaring parlor all to myself. I don't care how many of the family are present; it only gives piquancy to the progress of the acquaintance. Only give me a few dim nooks, like the shadow of a curtain, a bow window, or a projecting grand piano, with an occasional moonlight walk, and I'll get all the proposals I want, if I was two or three times a widow."

"You are a sensible woman, after my own heart. So you never sent your mother into the kitchen, and your sisters to bed, so as to have George all to yourself?"

" My mother would have boxed my ears had I proposed such a thing, and my father would have looked like a thunder cloud. We did enough courting to become acquainted, engaged, and married all within three months, and we had the novelty of finding out each other's best perfections afterwards ; not but that we found out a few little disagreeable qualities also; but that is better than knowing each other so well before marriage, that you can almost tell what each other is going to do and say from day to day. If I was a man I would marry no girl that threw her herself at my head, as it were, and would not accept me as a friend of the family, at least till I knew something of my own mind. I think this over-anxiousness to show a man you are ready to be married, is what prevents many men from even visiting families where there are young ladies, for fear they shall be looked upon as suitors, before they have ever made their third visit. The girls would fare better if they placed a higher value upon themselves, and remember they are more sensible, and really more charming in their twenties than in their bread-and-butter teens."

" Louisa, if ever you're a widow I'll—"

But she burst out laughing and said :

"Oh, yes, I know all about that. But I want you to come with me and show me George's tailor, for I am going to have a nice dress-ing gown made for him for a Christmas gift, and I want it to fit well, for he has such a handsome figure."

I put on my hat with a sigh. Ah ! why had I neglected my oppor-tunities in the arrogance of my young manhood ! Ah! why had I no fluttering earthly angel to minister to my wants, and think my figure handsome—echo answered why ?

Hop-o'-My-Thumb.

What Louisa thinks.

TO THE GIRLS OF TO-DAY.

I'm an old woman—an old, old woman; have buried three husbands and am carefully nursing the fourth in hopes of having somebody to bury me; still my faculties are as clear as ever, and I can see
a rent in a petticoat without my specs.

Now, girls, I want you all to come to me with your little joys and
sorrows, pleasures and disappointments, for I've had experience—a
whole library full. . Only think, four husbands! But that you'd call
me a cackling old hen, I'd give you the history of each.

Now, my dear girls, I know you are pretty, with the delicate peach
bloom—natural—still on your cheeks; I know you are smart, with
your high schools and colleges, and your drawing and music, and
though you think you know it all, more than your mother, grand-
mother and aunt combined, yet pause a moment and take the advice
of an old woman. I know its the one gift unappreciated, yet, often
when followed, worth millions. N. B.—Don't always follow it im-
plicitly when it concerns points in stocks, for once in a thousand it may
happen to be fallacious. You are willing, nay, eager, to accept
chocolate drops, gloves, gum, candy garters, in fact almost anything
that has a pecuniary value, yet unwilling to take what has cost years of
pain and trouble, care and solicitude—advice born of experience. I
know that advice in these days is like the aforesaid stocks—the bottom
is gone clean out, and it is not considered to be worth the assessment
of listening to. Yet did we not value the experiences of those who
lived before us, we should still believe the world to be flat, and the

long-tailed comet would cause the sinners among us to shriek in terror of utter annihiliation in a general smash up; but as it is, we serenely view his Ancient Terrorship through the most improved
glasses, and discuss the gasses of which he is composed. We are
thousands of years older—in knowledge I mean—than the ancients
just because we have had the sense to heed and make use of their
experiences; then why not take the experienced advice of one who
knows, especially when it concerns your domestic happiness? Now
all this is prefatory in hopes to induce you dear angels to listen to
Aunt Polly, and she says, "Girls, dear girls, don't marry too young."

Now, don't answer
this with a "pooh, pooh!"
"She married young, her-
self."   Yes, my dears,
I did; that's the reason
I can help you, for what
is more ridiculous than
a person trying to advise
on a subject they know
nothing about?   But
remember I have had
four husbands. You
think, no doubt, "Ah,
I'm different from other
people ; I shall manage
my husband." My dear,
women have thought so

This is before Marriage.

since the world began, but how many have succeeded ?

Look at the gaunt, hollow cheeks and the lines of dissatisfaction of
thousands of women who pass you in an afternoon's walk; do their
faces tell of mastership, or the utmost enjoyment of domestic bliss?

Rather don't they look as if they dare hardly call their souls their own ?'

When we are sweet sixteen, with no more sense than can be easily accommodated in our pretty heads, we are apt to think we are the motive power of the whole world. But let us begin at the beginning.

What is the first desire of nearly every newly married man ? Why a son and heir, not a daughter and heiress, you may be sure; and the poor, luckless little female who happens to be first of the family is to be pitied. So, you see, you almost come into the world uncalled for, unless two or three unruly boys precede you.

Why I heard the other day of a man who beat his wife, because their first happened to be a poor girly; and another, because the third was of the gentler sex when he wanted another boy; wouldn't speak to his wife for weeks. A word in your ear: I should think such a person would have nothing but girls, being so very unmanly.

Then think of the poor baby girls of China, India, and almost every heathen country. Think, also, of the countries nearer home; the son always inheriting first, the son always ruling first; the son, the son, always first in college, in business, in clothes. Look at this country; the son always President, always Senator, always Congressman, always voter, always almost everything—doctor, lawyer, soldier and sailor. Then you, a mere woman, four or five feet high, with a hundred or two of avoidupois, no trade, no profession, with perhaps, a pretty face, and a handsome pull-back, can rule a free-born man ! Why, the idea is preposterous.

Look what somebody said of Englishmen the other day. That they acquired their manly look of superiority and independence, by being master in their own houses; and I'll tell you what that means: I lived in that little island, myself, once.

" Jane," the wife, "brush my coat. Al, do up my shoes. Sallie. fasten my trousers straps under the shoes. Elizabeth, brush my hat," a stovepipe. "Maria, get my umbrella." And so he stands in the middle of the floor, his family flying about to obey with alacrity his slightest behest. I've helped, myself. Truly, an Englishman is boss of his own shanty.

When the young girl is about to escape from pinafores, has been to two picnics, one grown up party and a matinee, she thinks she is ready to be married. Why, a sixteen-year-older, who can neither read, write or cipher, told me to-day she was tired of this living single! And if a boy, with the down just appearing on his upper lip, has danced with her twice, squeezed her hand, and perhaps kissed her over the gate, she thinks she cannot live without him; that he is Apollo, Hercules and Jupiter combined; and if he has stooped for her fan, carried her parcels, and given her a box of gloves for a philopena, that he will make a most generous and devoted husband. Alas! she will find that after marriage she will go with holes in her gloves, and have no fan to pick up; and as for carrying parcels; how often have you seen the wife with the baby in her arms, the next hold

This is After Marriage.

of her dress, and a bag and bundle to boot, while her lord and master walks serenely ahead—just a foot or two—empty handed.

This is not uncommon, for I speak by the card. But this is the least you'll have to complain of. Remember, all men—custom says so —must sow their wild oats ; of course there are some exceptions ; my third, for instance, was a most exemplary man ; so that if you marry such a young man ; who has not had time to sow the aforesaid oats before marriage, he'll find, or make time to engage in that delightful —to him—occupation, after. But that's no guide for your actions, he'll soon let you know ; for do you look twice at the same man, or ride quietly to see the seals, as he thinks nothing of doing, and he'll let you know who boards and clothes you.

Does he think the house ever gets tedious to you, as it does to him in less than a half hour consecutive stay in it, and offer to take you for a walk or drive ? Not much. I've been married years upon years, yet even my exemplary third only mildly hinted at it once, when I looked pale and tired, and called his attention to the fact ; in all our other walks together, I led him like a lamb to the slaughter, with a re-signed look upon his dear face, pathetic by its patience, especially if we were accompanied by our ninth. So if you marry young, you're apt to have your ninth or tenth before your hair is gray, and not to have visited the next county to you unless allowed to by your devoted, who doesn't go himself and can have such a jolly time while you are away, playing bachelor. Bend down your head. Don't you go, at least alone.

How many parties do you think your beloved will take you to after the ceremony ? Make the most of that ceremony, for it will be the last in which you are the observed of all observers, unless you happen to become a widow several times.

"Why don't you bring your wife, Will ?"

"Oh, the old woman's at home minding the baby. She's always got a baby to mind." The last part in a sneering and contemptuous tone. Or if there's no baby, alack and alas ! it is worse still, for then it is the lodge—the perennial lodge, claims him almost body and soul, and he pays you in neglect for the many jokes a childless married man has to endure. And don't you dare ask him where he's been and why he's been, or he may answer you as my fourth paralyzed me with :

"I want none of your chin music about it, either !"

I could have fainted, but I was in bed, and could thus make no sensation falling in his arms, so I swallowed my wrath. But there, I've done for to-day. Another time I'll tell you how I managed my exemplary third, with the experience gained, alas, and felt, by my two former experiments.

Be patient, dear girls, and don't marry till you hear from me again.

Hop-o'-My-Thumb.

What Aunt Polly knows.

A LOQUACIOUS WOMAN.

Heaven defend me from a loquacious woman! for heaven alone can; no artifice, no seclusion of yours can accomplish the desired end unless strong bolts and bars divide you, then I do believe she would cackle through the door.

Oh, I am almost sick and weary of life. I'm getting to despise the sex; to think it's only idiots who marry, and fools who help to multiply the race, and all on account of not one fair woman, but one loquacious ditto.

Will her tongue never cease till the coffin covers her, or will that be insufficient till six feet of solid earth adds its pressure ?

Married men, I pity you, if this woman is a sample of her sex.

Should you hang, drown and shoot yourself all at the same time, and should your end be annihilation, still it would be a blissful change from the eternal chatter, chatter, chatter, cackle, cackle, cackle, buss, buss, buss, burr, burr-r-r-r-r.

I've just got acquainted with one, and I'm to be pitied; I did not believe such a thing existed in this world or the next. I immure myself in a book and pretend not to hear, but, " Don't you think so ?" is reiterated louder and louder, till you must answer, or your nerves would sting you to death.

" How much did it cost ?" " Have you had it long ?" " Does any body else wear that style ?" " Has Mr. Smith had his girl long ? Does she get out often ? Does she sleep alone ? What does she get ?" Just as though I was a walking compendium of the private affairs of the whole neighborhood. Oh, good gracious! but wont she revenge the wrongs of her sex! Yes, ten thousand of them. I can now see the ghastly, grim reality of the joke, " This man was talked to death!" illustrated with a coffin and cross bones, displayed on a man's lappel when he wishes to be rid of a bore. I would almost have one photographed on my forehead, if this woman would take the hint; but alas! these kind of people will take your time, your tea, your cake, but they won't take your hints, asking your opinion on all their little petty affairs, that you don't care a blank for, that you've got no opinion about, and wouldn't have for almost any money.

I wouldn't blame the husband of such a wife for seeking oblivion in the bowl, or resting his nerves in the corner grocery in a quiet game of whist, or driving to the Cliff House to watch the seals, or,— but no; he'll never seek the society of females; his one is more than enough; it's full measure and running over.

How a person's tongue can be their greatest enemy and other people's also!

I once knew a gentleman that I thought it would be quite a task for any lady to beat in talking, but he did say something once in a while. But this woman begins when she opens her eyes, and keeps it up till blessed sleep seals her tongue, and still she says nothing.

You can't get rid of her, either. Did you ever have a burr stick to your clothing when you went into the fields? She is a burr; you can't get rid of her; if you go into another room, she soon follows; if you go into the garden she is there; if you don't answer it's all the same; she talks, talks, talks, for the ineffable pleasure of hearing her own voice.

Now I know it's pleasant to converse with a woman when she has a few ideas back of her magnificent eyes, but even such a one should be chary of her visits and words; never satiate a person however much you may like them, and they like you; it's well to have even your husband desire you should say more, than wish you had not said so much.

And it's this loquacity that causes so much of the scandal and misery of the world; no harm was meant, but oh, the women do love to talk; they would die with out it, as I once heard a little boy who was very hoarse say:

" I'd rather be dead, than not to talk!"

But oh, woman, gentle woman, don't drive one distracted; don't make them wish that either they or you were never born; there's time enough in three score years and ten to say a good deal; don't try to compress it all in three score minutes. Be warned—be advised by one who has had his nerves tingling, and was ready to commit almost any crime by being condemned to share the house for three weeks with a fearful, gingling, maddening, loquacious woman. Pray for me.

                                        Hop-o'- M y-Thumb.

Frank's experience.

THE BABY.

We've all been it—the bright, the beautiful baby, the ootsie-tootsie, mamma's darling; the prettiest, sweetest, dearest little bit of mortality that ever graced long clothes and had the colic.

"Yes, you've all been it !" murmurs the growler, not always the old bachelor, but sometimes the young one, who imagines that he came into the world with pants on, or was of such an angelic disposition that he never cried when the pins were running into him half an inch, or when he was trotted till every bone in his body semed to be having an earthquake ; or when he was so hungry that he felt he could eat his very fingers if they were only sugared a little.

But he—the growler—dosen't think it—the baby—the brightest, prettiest thing, especially if he is left to mind it for an hour or two while its own dear mamma goes down town to do a little shopping. I know of one young bachelor who crammed its mouth with green silk, and not finding that soporific, held its head downward, and finding it objected to that, let it squall out its dear little lungs till its mother rescued it. Ah ! he forgot that he was once a little old precious, and cried like the rest of them; yet he had no mouth crammed with green silk; he hadn't been held in an inverted ratio; he remembered only that he didn't like babies, at least when they cried. They were all very well in pictures, or sculptured as Cupid, or smiling in their mother's arms, especially if she was young and pretty.

Of course, it is not so pleasant when it cries for two or three hours with no let up; still it gives a very good idea of perpetual motion and it is well to utilize everything.

Yet, what is home without a baby? with no little feet pattering music on the floor, with no little lips lisping pearl drops, that gladdens every mother heart?

Many love them best when they are in long clothes and just beginning to smile ; but that's the time the crusty bachelor, old or young—the bachelor at heart, I mean, and some married men are that—think they are limbs of Satan, and says so too.

"They are only sent to worry the life out of respectable married men, and keep sensible single ones from following their example." It's all very well to say you won't walk the floor at night, no matter how it squalls, and even stipulate to that effect before matrimony; but when the cash runs short, and you are blessed—that's ironical—with twins, what wouldn't you do to stop their howling? and they always tune up just when you're sleepiest—at least the General tells me so; and gossips do say, that as he brushes by the Venetian blinds they sometimes turn and disclose a ghost-like figure in white, with naked extremities, a baby in each arm, singing jovial songs in a stentorian voice, as a counter-irritant, you know, with a face of perfect misery, and hair in wild disorder."

This is the General.

The young mother who knows better, says she don't believe it; her hubby can sleep through the stormiest squall her two can make and though they are not twins they are nearly so. Then old Crusty wants to know why they weren't born without colic, any how, as that can't be for their ultimate beatification. But this is a question the mother can't answer, at least satisfactory to one who is worried nearly to the verge of madness by Mrs. Jones' cross baby next door. The excuse of an apple ate by the mother, or a dish of cabbage, or pork and beans, causes a sarcastic smile on the face of the Doubter, who thinks it their true inwardness that must have vent, or the machinery burst. (Hush! sometimes the fond mother thinks it's a little that way herself, but she wouldn't for the world say so.)

Once upon a time there was a man, and he was a newspaper man, and a very foolish young man, for he wrote and published a fearful, dreadful, terrible slur on babies, and could the aforesaid have risen in force they would have annihilated him, but owing to their weakness, their mothers took up their cause and just deluged that paper office with letters; emphatic, ironic, choleric, in fact of every angry description, till the editor had to utter a protest; but worst of all many threatened to stop their paper, so a compromise had to be effected; a pretty poem "To the Baby," published, or something. It doesn't do to offend the women, and you can't do it more effectually than by disparaging the baby.

Of course we can't see the faults of our own five-year-older, and think it is that hateful Mrs. Smith's boy that will always begin a fight with our darling, and the aforesaid hateful thinks it's just the same with her hopeful. Well, if we didn't think so, who would care for the ugly and uninteresting; but that, you know, isn't their fault; they would all be beautiful and smart if they could. So Heaven has planted this beautiful, beautiful mother-love in the hearts of women, so that they can endure fatigue, worry, loss of sleep, hunger, cold, almost without a murmur, for baby's sake; and when it sickens, how the mother's heart feels every pain intensified, and when it dies who can comfort ?

Close the eyes and fold the little hands; put away the clothes and little shoes that the restless little feet have worn red and shining. Weep fond mother, weep, or your heart will break. God gave you tears; it is not wicked to shed them over the loss of this precious gift—your loved little baby. It is so hard, so hard to part with it. The beauty, the joy, the brightness seems gone out of your life, now the lisping tongue is silent. You sit and moan, and moan and moan, till the other children weep to hear you. How cold and white your little darling is. You never took his hand before that he did not reward you with a smile, a kiss, or a pretty word. But now, he does not notice you. O, God I if it should be thus in the other world; if he should not recognize his mother who so loved him, so suffered for him ; if he should not run to meet her— then were Heaven a place of torment, instead of eternal bliss; but God is too good to blast a mother's hopes. You will meet your baby there, poor mother, and it will know you and love you far better than it did on earth. It has only gone on a journey to a more beautiful country, where there is no pain; it will wait for you, and when you cross the dark river, it will not be a strange land your feet will touch, for baby will be there to welcome you.

LIBERTY.

There is no such thing as liberty for man, woman, or child. As he is born, so is his destiny thrust upon him. It is all sophistry to say a man can carve out his own destiny; a man can do this, and a man can do that, but it begins and ends with saying a man can do. Does any one ever say a woman can carve out her own destiny?

If a woman is a slave—and the proof shill yet be shown that she is still in the worst of bondage—a man is also, but differently, and more to his own satisfaction.

Who ever heard of a great man arising out of the scum of St. Giles? We know that this poet's father was a shoemaker, or small tradesman;

that that great-divine came, perhaps, from a tailor shop, and that this great statesman, and that successful general were of common-place, but respectable parents.

But who ever heard of the son of a sot—not a man who takes even half a dozen drinks a day, but a drunkard—who has lost all sense of moral obligation while his child is still in his adolescence, or the son of a thief, who from earliest childhood has been taught the height of ambition was to be able to crack a crib successfully without detection? who ever heard of such men's sons becoming great or good or even respectable? Yet were they given the choice of St. James or St. Giles? or whether their fathers should be princes or paupers?

We will assume that the sot's son has perfect liberty, but what is it to him but an empty sound? With no education to raise his thoughts above the animal instincts of food and warmth; with no experience to show him, that outside those disgusting purlieus are brave, good men, beautiful, loving women, noble deeds, great achievements, a world so different from his own, that could he understand it, 'twould appear like a bright fairy tale. But he is shut out from all this, almost as effectually as if he were confined behind the bars of a prison cell. Lack of intelligence, lack of appreciation, lack of money—these are his jailors.

And these same jailors jealously guard the prison homes of millions more besides the sons of sots and thieves. We look in vain for a remedy.

"Education, education, education!" is the cry, but we must go with the strong arms of giants, and seize these children bodily; for they will not seek voluntarily that of which they know nothing; and the weak parents—weak with ignorance, or poverty, or rum, say:

" Look at us; we didn't never have any teachin'; it didn't harm us."

* So each degraded father and mother leaves duplicates and triplicates of themselves to follow in their miserable footsteps, and yet we talk of liberty!

Even custom, though it often goes against our common sense, is strong enough to make us do ridiculous things, though we profess to despise both fashion and custom; yet it restrains our free instincts as chains of iron would the free use of our limbs.

Is there one of us independent enough to do just as he pleases? And if so, what does he become? A hoodlum, pure and simple.

The nearest approach to liberty is when the boy of six or seven sneaks off from school and plays the truant; then his evil passions are dormant, and his only thoughts are for enjoyment; true, he runs the risk of being drowned, run over, a bloody nose or a black eye, and the awful fear of the paternal chastisement, when the inevitable night comes, looms up ominously, like a dark cloud momentarily obscuring his pleasure; but he finally makes up his mind to bear it bravely, and then puts all disagreeable thoughts from his mind; and this is the nearest we come to liberty!

One man, or rather thousands, are the slaves of Pedro, casino, whist, faro, etc.; another of tobacco, or opium; others, money-getting; others wine; others yet, of ambition. Again we ask, "What remedy?" The answer is an echoed and re-echoed "what?"

A man is born a slave, and will die a slave, and Bob Ingersoll won't save him.   HOP O'-MY-THUMB.

What Katie thinks.

GRIEVANCES.

Is a woman happy without a grievance? You gentlemen will say no; and I almost think you are right. The dull monotony of a woman's life must be broken by something; if it be not a grievance, it must be excitement, and one can imagine the great excitement of minding children, mending clothes, with an occasional book to read; sometimes washing dishes and cooking besides; not even the excitement of marketing is allowed most women, where the stalls of bright vegetables and flowers, and clean looking meat stretch for miles, and one can have the excitement of meeting most of their acquaintances, without the trouble of visiting, and indulging in the current gossip, getting it fresh every morning.

Without something to complain of a woman would be too happy for this world; she would be ready to die, and willing, too, most like. How could she exercise the spice of original sin inherited from Mother Eve? If she couldn't fret and scold a wee little bit, her husband would be most unhappy finding he had married a saint when he supposed he had married a woman. His own little deficiencies would become so great by comparison, that he would sigh for the shrill voice and the occasional biscuit thrown at his head, to be able to draw up a better balance sheet.

If the husband is an angel then again there is trouble in the camp, for he doesn't afford the least opportunity for the excitement of a quarrel; so the children stand in his stead, and are the worst in the world.

" He's the worst boy! I can't do anything with him; other children 'll mind, but he—" I heard a woman say, and he was her grievance, and perhaps prevented her other half from getting an undue amount of Caudle lectures.

If it wasn't for the servant-girl question, some women's lives would stagnate, especially during the fashionable morning calls. Oh, the grief they cause them with their waste, their tea parties, and their laziness! And, oh, the good it does them to talk about it.

Some women are at their happiest when they are deepest in trouble. When things run smoothly and they are not even in debt, they see nothing to live for, and wonder why they were born.

Why I know a lady who is so well off that she has everything she wishes for; and yet she is not happy, but makes a grievance of her neighbors; and if Mr. Jones does not treat his horse or his wife just as he ought to, why her brow is corrugated, and she looks as if she had the weight of the world on her shoulders.

Oh! happy the woman who has a dozen children, not much money, and no time to think her life monotonous, and needs no grievance as an outlet for her superfluity of feeling.

Oh! happy the woman who brings to her husband a mother-in-law, and lots of relations-in-law so that his very occasional visits to the corner do not make her so lonely that she wishes herself dead, and she finds that life is still endurable if her husband does play "Pedro" for the drinks, and sometimes loses too many games for his equilibrium.

Why, some women make a grievance of their fine furniture, and moan if the dust blows in too thickly, or run to tears if the head of the house accidentally mistakes the carpet for the cuspador! I've known them, so have you, and who act as if sitting on pins if a friend brings in a young hopeful of an enquiring mind, who wishes to look at the books, or at the bric-a-brac on the what-not or grown-up people's toy box that stands in the corner.

Some grieve because they are so fat that their pull-back does not set them off to the best advantage, and pinch and squeeze, and try the Banting system, to reduce their avoirdupoise. Some make a grievance of their very lack of this same carbon, and the object of their life is to drink ale and porter and eat rare beef to accomplish the wished-for augmentation.

Some sigh because their locks are dark, when fashion calls for blonde; some because their clothes are not just in the style; but, oh! the grievance of all grievances, is the husband! His every fault is canvassed, even to the slightest, and some women make confidants of every one who will lend a pitying ear. He neglects his home—he drinks; he looks too often at that brazen Miss Smith; he don't dress her fine enough, but wastes his money on filthy tobacco; he—he—he. But if she is discreet and keeps his failings to herself, she thinks, "What shall I scold him about when he comes home?" Not exactly in these words, but rather—

''On what subject do we need reform?" And if the husband is sensible he'll let her reform him to her heart's content; it might prevent her having fever by allowing vent to her pent-up feelings. Don't be silly and get mad. Remember, gentlemen, you've had a dozen opportunities during the day of d—, or rather blanking somebody; your clerk, or your porter, or the stocks, while your poor wife has had, perhaps, no one on whom she had a legitimate right to exercise her vocal organ. How would you like to pass a whole day without being allowed to utter strong language? It would almost kill some gentlemen I know. Sympathize, therefore, with your loving wives, and sacrifice yourselves for a few moments for their peace of mind.

"Yes, my dear, you are right; I'll reform." With these sweet words in her ear, she'll sleep peacefully, thinking she has not lived in vain.

This is the Quarrel.

Happy the woman who has an in-growing nail, or the neuralgia, or a prize puzzle to decipher; some real grievance, so that the innocent might not suffer; and happy the woman who is not so perfect, and whose husband is not such an angel but that they can get up a good old-fashioned quarrel once in a while, so that healthy excitement may not fade out of their lives, and they die all too soon out of *ennui*, leaving their little ones a sad monument of the desolation caused by two persons not having a single grievance.

What Lucy don't think.

Hop-o'-My-Thumb.

WOMAN---NO. 2.

I never saw a woman yet who did not regret being born a woman; I never saw a woman yet who did not wish she were a man; I never saw a woman yet who did not feel that the conventionalities that environed her were too circumscribed for the full development of her heart and brain; I never saw a woman but would make a better man than half the so-called creatures that wear the bifurcated. *And yet I am a woman;* but my consent was never asked whether I should be a ruler, or be ruled; my consent was never asked whether the limited (in some respects unlimited) duties of a house would satisfy all the cravings of my intellect, as well as heart; I was never given the choice of being a woman, and have the easy and delicious task of bearing

and rearing a large family, or being a mighty man, and with the
strength demanding, intellect developing occupation of selling hose
and chemises to ladies; I was never consulted whether I should be a
President or be a pot-washer, there being no act of mine that I was
born this poor, despicable, unloved thing—a woman—and no act of
his that Nature placed him on the unlimited throne of manhood;
then what calls for the extra consideration, respect and deference paid
him even from his birth? They say that in this country women are
so free, women are so carefully tended, women are so adored (?); that
in rough Germany they are harnessed to carts and to the plow; that
they lose all the sweet bloom of womanhood, etc., etc. I myself
have seen, in the quaint city of Quebec, a woman and a dog harnessed together, drawing a cart. Here, you see, they do more than
a man. He guides the plow, he drives the horse or dog, he is master,
but never equal; that would be degrading. True, I don't want women to pitch brick and carry the hod, as the women in Antwerp; yet
even to do this, even to draw the plow, or pull the cart, there are
some advantages; God's glorious sky, His waving grain, His life-giv-
ing perfumed air are familiar things, ever surrounding her, not coveted
and yearned for in vain, as the pale-faced sewing woman, or the poor
woman of many children, alas ! knows how. They, too, have the
satisfaction of knowing that they earn their bread. We know there
are happy women, contented women, who are satisfied with just what
they are and just what they have. They need no emancipation. I
am writing in the cause of the oppressed, the ground down, the bitterly
unhappy. Yet for them there is only partial alleviation, never perfect
while man remains man, and woman woman, and even the theory of
"evolution" does not teach that in the blessed progress of humans
and things, the sexes will be changed.

We know that women hate each other—with exceptions, of course—
we know that it is called naughty, unwomanly, etc., but *we* know that

it is natural; we know our little peculiarities born of *being* a woman; we know the vapid, useless, tiresome lives so many lead, where the father or husband has a little more than is necessary to live from hand to mouth. We know the hopeless, sunless work and worry of those who have less.

When men compare this country with European nations, they forget the parks and gardens, where many of the women that otherwise would scarcely see the sunlight, the trees and flowers, take their children, their lunch and sewing, and spend many happy, contented days.

They forget the innumerable petty shop-keepers, where the wife is half the firm, and does business like a man. Here, if a woman tries to make money in stocks, taking no more illegetimate means than a man does, oh, she's a mud-hen! Such a term! Yet they sicken of women book-peddlers, and won't buy patent button-fasteners; so if the woman happens to be a widow, or without support, and is not a servant or shop-woman—and those places are overrun, for there must be some to buy and some to work for—then how does a man expect her to earn her bread, and that, perhaps, of her dependent children ? When she first tried to be a type-setter, how she was sneered at and reviled. And even now they have not ceased to scandalize the female treasury clerks, although, after all these years of trial, not one has been found dishonest. Men say, sneeringly, they haven't the courage (?). It is a pity, so their mothers think, that they have, for any one can be a villian; the lowest scuff and scum can be a thief. It is the courageous man who is honest, though sorely tempted by want.

The men sneer at each advance in the progress of women's labor, fearing their own stability. Look at the school question—women paid less for the same work. Such rank injustice, to make discrimination in the sex of brains

Men forget that in France women always rule, first by their youth and beauty, then by their intellect, last by their piety. They forget when they boast of glorious America, the paradise of women, that it is a paradise only for the tender greenlings. Society is for the girls in heir teens, where a woman over thirty is voted a bore; they don't want " old folks," so precocious is their hot-house growth. How different in Europe; every lady who has traveled—being past the bread and butter age—will tell. Alack and alas! we in America need much reconstruction. We ask for a more enlarged life for women, for a broader field of occupation; give them every little concession possible to add to their happiness; their homes should be places to help equa l the freedom of enjoyment the men posess as a divine (?) right.

We only ask that they shall not be so stinted in the pay for their work, either for others or their husbands, that they shall constantly feel as if they were living on sufferance and their necessary clothing a divine favor for which they could not enough thank God—and their husbands!

Hop-o'-My-Thumb.

What Madeline believes.

UTILIZING THE RICH

I was sitting in my office meditating on the mutability of human affairs—we always meditate on this subject when we have more time than money—when a quick, decided little step approached the door, and a lively little drum beat, played by the back of two fingers, sounded on the glass pane ; it was Tom's wife, I knew, so I cried :

"Come in !" in the sweetest voice I could command, and when she appeared, I greeted her with a great deal of enthusiasm—for I had not seen her for some time—shaking her hands and seating her in my big chair; then, for the first time, I noticed she had no smile upon her face.

"Oh! Uncle John, I've got the blues!" she cried, throwing back her head and dropping the seal skin cap upon the floor.

" You ?"

, " Yes, but thank goodness not for myself this time."

"Relieve your mind, my dear, and tell me all about it," I said, patting her hands in a fatherly way.

"Well, you see, Mrs. Jones—I call her Mrs. Jones, Uncle John, so that you shall not know who I mean—well, she is going to have another baby!" I wondered in my mind why that should give her the blues but said nothing.

"You see she has nine children already, and it takes all her time to attend to their wants, and darn her husband's stockings—oh, he does wear such big holes in them, she showed me—that she has none for herself; can't visit or attend the matinees, and I should so like to have her go with me, for she is very lively, and the soul of wit, whatever that may be."

"Still, my dear, I can't see why this should give you the blues," I ventured to remark.

" Don't you see she is fulfilling the Divine command, and yet Providence don't seem to be helping her out the least bit, any more— no, not as much—than as if she was breaking it; and she said to me; " If Heaven will keep sending the little ones—oh, you needn't laugh, Uncle John, for she said no matter how much people laughed and sneered at the idea, especially those who had none, that Heaven, and nobody but Heaven, sent them. Witness the fact that they who are childless, might beg in vain till they were gray, for one little likeness of themselves, while somebody else, who would be contented with half-a-dozen, is presented with nine or ten."

"My dear, you have wandered from the point," I said. "You spoke of Heaven sending the little ones."

"Oh, yes! She said she thought that Heaven might send plenty of means to take good care of them. 'There's Mr. Robinson,' she continued, 'without chick or child, and so wealthy that he don't know what to do with his money. Why, his stable, even, is finer than our house; and when my Jack wants a coat, and Angeline a petticoat, and Mary Walker Beatrice a chimeloon, and Grant Lee—you see, I'm neutral in politics—a pair of warm stockings, I'm apt to think Heaven hasn't distributed the goods of this world just right.'"

I wished to ask her what that "loon" something was, but was afraid to.

"'Oh, I don't mind having nine children,' she continued, 'for the love comes with them, and I wouldn't lose one for all Mr. Robinson's wealth; but I don't like to lose all my sleep at night by having four in the bed, because they will sleep with their mamma and papa. Now, if I even had a mother-in-law with me, she would take charge of a few, for she would not allow 'my son's' children to be neglected, and seeing that I had but two knees and two arms, and could accommodate but three at the most, comfortably, would take pity on me; but having only one girl to do all the work and washing, when night comes she is almost as worn out and tired as myself; but then, she can have her night's sleep,' she added, with a sigh, 'and that is what I miss.'"

I no longer wondered that Tom's wife had the blues; I was beginning to feel that color myself, but I put on a cheerful countenance and said:

"Well, what did she suggest as a remedy?"

"Rather a novel one; to tax all the rich people who had no children, and the proceeds to be distributed equally *per capita*—is that

right, Uncle John?—among those who had over three, whether rich or
poor, so that accepting it should not be receiving charity. This would
relieve a great deal of suffering and save many lives, for sometimes
those apparently well-to-do, have not enough money at times to buy
needed medicines and attendance for their sick little ones, or comforts
enough for their well. But there, we have no hand in making the
laws if we do have all the babies. She's my friend, Uncle John, and
I can't bear to think of the additional trouble she'll soon have on her
hands; those two babies crying at once, for her youngest can't walk or
talk, constantly with one in her arms, and sometimes the two. Oh, I
can see her now in imagination. Then sitting up in bed shivering
rocking the baby, so it shan't disturb the other, and that the rest of
them—and 'them' her dear husband, so she prefers to suffer alone; oh,
she's done it before; I know her."

I suggest a good nurse.

"That's it! You see they can't afford one; she doesn't wish to deprive her husband of all his little enjoyments, his Pedro, cigars, etc.,
not wanting him to wish he was a bachelor again; so, though he
spends more than enough to keep a good nurse or even his mother-
in-law, still she keeps a cheerful face, and grows old and broken down
silently. Now you see if the rich were taxed, that would be entirely
for the benefit of the mother and children, so that she need not interfere with his little pleasures, and still have some of her own. Uncle
John, you're a man and a part of the government; now can't you
petition Congress, or whoever in Washington does such things, to pass
such a law? That's what I came to see you about this morning.
You're so talented and eloquent, that it would be no trouble at all to
you."

I blushed up to my eyes. I felt it, to have a young and pretty
woman thus compliment me.

"You see, Uncle John, they say, at least I heard a young man say once, speaking of his father :

"'Well, what did he bring me into the world for ? I didn't ask him to.' He forgot that his father didn't ask his paternal to do that office, or his, his, and so on till you come to Adam; so that he should blame God, which he would not dare to do. Then suppose there were no more children born, as so many growlers and children-haters wish, where would this world be in fifty years, or rather, what would it be ? The cities silent and almost uninhabited, the plough rusting in the furrow, the grass growing in the canals and corn fields, the humming machinery broken and decayed, the printing press silent and unused, the telegraph poles cut up for fire wood, no smile upon a human face, each one fearing in horror to be the 'Last Man.' 'Tis easy enough to advance in years with our children growing up around us, keeping the busy wheels of commerce, education and the fine arts ever active, still progressive, but to wait till death comes, without a child's voice or smile to gladden us, to look only into faces old with sorrow and care; to see everything decaying and dying around us, must be terrible indeed, so why do those smart one, some of them not out of their teens, look upon babies as nuisances, and think it would be best for the world if no more we born, when it would be death, hideous death for this glorious beautiful paradise we inhabit. Only, things ought to be distributed a little more evenly."

I was silent; Her eloquence subdued me. But as she seemed waiting for me to speak, I at last suggested sending them to the Foundling Asylum; but she burst out crying.

"Oh, Uncle John, I did not expect that of you. I may be a mother myself some day, and—and—" but her sobs choked her utterance. Now, here was a dilemma! I did not know how to comfort her, not having had any experience in the subject; and as her sobs became louder and louder, I no longer wondered how they could rule their busbands, for I would have done anything to have stopped the heart-rending sound.

This is the Petition.

"Maggie!" I cried, "dear Maggie.   I'll do it. I'll get up a petition a mile long, signed with a hundred thousand names, and send it to Washington!" Her sobs stopped; a smile broke over her countenance, and throwing her arms around me, she cried:

"Thou woman's friend! Bless you, bless you!"

And that is the reason I carry this parchment and know every married man and woman in town. .

Hop-o'-My-Thumb.

This is Maggie's opinion.

———

THE MAN WHO STAYS AT HOME TOO MUCH.

Tell it not in Gath; speak it not in—whatever the quotation may be—that I've been eating onions! But this is my beloved husband's day out, so he'll never know it. You see, my other half is an author, poet, dramatist, etc.; but his principal business is writing for a newspaper, and he has just finished his weekly masterpiece, blacked his shoes, put on a clean shirt, left a thousand and one directions as to what we shall all do during his absence, kissed his son and heir, shook his hand to baby, just touched my lips as gently as a Summer's breeze, said "ta, ta," to the girls, and jumped into the car, or, rather, upon it, for he stands on the platform as long as the house is in sight.

Well, I've been eating onions; the fact is, we've all been eating them, except the baby, for the girls say they don't expect their beaux to-night, as it is Saturday, and they spend nearly all Sunday with them, so they'll just have a feast—Spanish, large and raw at that.

Thus you see the effect of liberty. My beloved will return at six P. M., by the clock. Let me see, it will be a little past by ours, as it is always fast. Well, he will return with a renewed lease of life for another week; that is to say, he will go to the office, get his little stipend, then, after chatting a few moments with the gentlemanly book-keeper, he will make straight for a barber shop, have his beautiful, poetic long hair—my pride—clipped to the dimensions of ordinary mortals, and his week's beard, which made him look so dirty and cross, removed to the roots; have his moustache curled *á la* Napoleon, and a little delicate perfumery sprayed over his distinguished coun-tenance; then, with a little brushing up, he will come from that shop a renewed man. From there he goes—he has often given me his pro-gramme minutely—not to the Fountain, but to the place near it—and plays his weekly three games of Pedro—not for the drinks, as he plays with a trio of geniuses like himself, who can hardly afford it, though they do take it in turns each week, to do the generous and pay for one round of cigars. Then he goes to the most fashionable tailor, in-quires the price of their handsomest suit; how long it would take to make him a duplicate—there is nothing like putting on a little style, he tells me—buys a box of paper collars and—but I wont tire out in-dulgent patience with too much minuteness; suffice it to say he ends at the market, where he always purchases an extra fine dinner for Sunday, for my poet loves his stomach like a common man.

And I, in the mean time? Well, I go in my old rags and drop my back hair; the girls take off their 'attire.' 'Sh ! their bustles, and in-dulge in onions; the son and heir eats molasses with his fingers and makes sand pies. The baby is allowed the luxury of a little bawl— she's a girl, it won't hurt her—and we're all as happy as kings.

Now, don't think we are unappreciative of the great mind that

Heaven has kindly granted to be our constant companion, and the
father of our dear girls, *et al;* it's the "constant," there's the rub.
There is a neighbor of mine whose husband is Falstaffian and good
natured, who would almost give her little finger for him to have a
moiety of the stay-at-home qualities of my beloved, but he runs the
"primaries" at the corner groceries. "That's the place to fetch 'em,"
he tells her, and he is weighty at city elections ; can influence just
nineteen and a half votes—the half is the man who stood on the
fence. His candidates are not always successful, but that's not his
fault. After a hurried breakfast, to eat which she has sent over half the
neighborhood to all the "primaries," she sees him no more till whatever hour of the night or morning his important political duties release him. She goes to sleep with her head on the table waiting for
him ; she stands at the window in her nightgown, like a ghos' ; she
naps on the hard sofa till she gets a crick in the neck ; she reads over
the scraps of paper the bread comes in (he doesn't subscribe for a paper,
he reads it all at the "primaries"); she does everything to pass the
weary time away, and yet she is not happy. Of course, it's one thing
to be too much one way, and it's pretty much the same to be too
much the other way. But, to return to our mutton—or, rather, beef—
for that's what our beloved generally buys, a great big roast, for that's
the cheapest, and really good, and makes excellent hash, (he's so
thoughtful); then there's a variety of vegetables—they're cheap—and
a variety of fruit. The girls are always glad when Saturday comes,
for, besides the good things and their father's improved appearance,
they get the delightful, the entertaining, the loved Sunday paper,
which they eagerly devour all the week. They send the son and heir,
who doesn't love onions, to their paternal to ask for the paper to read
his piece. This flatters him, so they always get it, after he has taken
a cursory glance at his own effort and that of his rival.

Geniuses are seldom rich, so my beloved's study is the dining room, so we make the kitchen do double duty, except on Sunday and State occasions ; nevertheless, he sees everything, hears everything, knows everything—how many pairs of stockings the girls possess, whether they are darned or not ; if they have let their beaux squeeze their hands or kiss them, on the sly ; how many of my white petticoats are in the wash, protesting against the fluted ones as useless extravagance ; how many times I change the baby's undershirt ; scolds when we are in a hurry and hide the dishes under the sink. Nothing is hid from his Argus eyes till we really sometimes wish that he would play Pedro a little more, or would begin a great play, that would absorb all his faculties, hearing, sight and smell. Then we wouldn't keep the baby forever on the trot, so as not to disturb his reveries ; then we could sing out of time, or even out of tune, without his noticing it ; go with holes in our stockings, or even bustleless ; the dear girls could have their beaux more nights in the week than one, and we could make molasses candy undisturbed and eat onions in the kitchen. Ye nine Muses, send him an inspiration, is the prayer of three grown up females.

Hop-o-My-Thumb.

Katie's secret.

HOW A WOMAN KEPT SECRET.

The tedium of my office was enlivened the other day by the entrance of Marian. Now Marian has black eyes. And when she laughs you can imagine how pleasant it is to see and hear her.

"Oh! Nunky!" she said as she sank into my great leather chair— this is an affectionate term many of my female friends use in address-

ing me, their advisor and counsellor—"I have just read in the paper
that a woman can't keep a secret—"

''Of course they cannot, that is a known fact, and the newspapers
never lie!'' I replied.

"So I thought, but for once they are mistaken." She said with a
merry twinkle in her eye. "For I've kept a secret from my husband
for—let me see—yes, six years; Oh! it was nothing he'd be ashamed
to hear, so you need not look at me so enquiringly."

"My child, I was only thinking that six years was a very long time
to keep a secret."

"It might be sixty before he knows it, as I might never tell him."

I began to think she might never tell me, also; but as men have no
curiosity, I only felt that I should like to know in the interest of science.

"Uncle John, do you think a woman tells her husband eyerything?
if they did it would make a great deal of mischief, and for what use?
perhaps to make their husband and his best friend mortal enemies; because forsooth, he told his friend's wife that she looked ever so charming; or, pressed her fingers with one millioneth part of a horse power
more than was absolutely necessary in an ordinary shaking of hands;
oh dear! no! we are wiser than that, for which of our beloveds comes
home and says what a pleasant little flirtation he had with Mrs. or
Miss So-and-So; or, how he gave her a ten cent bunch of violets which
his own wife would have thought an inestimable present, presaging
the return of love's young dream, etc."

"Oh, child! married men never do such things," I replied when
I could get the chance.

"You are right. They never do—that is, bring violets home to
their wife."

Misunderstood—but that is man's fate.

Was she never going to divulge that six years' secret? Were the newspapers wrong after all?

"So you have not told your husband yet," I said in an encouraging tone.

"No; if I had informed him too soon, it might have brought all my trouble back, strongly reinforced."

What trouble could she have had that she dreaded so? She with the bright black eyes; but I was getting impatient, and after what seemed to me two hours and a half of tantalizing, I put the leading question:

"Well, my dear, what was it?"

"Oh, I haven't told you yet, have I? Well, you see, William was very fond of dogs—"

Pshaw! only about a dog, after all—I thought.

"And as we lived in a city where there was plenty of yard room, he indulged his fondness to the bent, first in a dear New Foundland pup, to bring up on the bottle; 'he will be *such* a beauty,' " Will said:

I looked disconsolately at the twins, and the little fellow just walking, and sighed. But the pup must be cared for, whether or no; so I bottled him till he was weaned, and he really was very pretty, but oh! so mischievous. The baby clothes he tore was enough to last a little one a year; so I told Will, but he would only smile and excuse him. One day a friend came and took a great fancy to the dog, and after begging very hard, Will finally gave him to him. How glad I was! But my joy was of short duration, for the very next day two pups—a greyhound and a mongrel—at their most mischievous age, were brought to fill the vacancy! and so it went on for years, as fast as one pup got to be worth anything, a friend begged him and one, two, or three more were brought to take his place. My protests were all in vain; the ruined clothes were replaced with a smile and my life was a species of purgatory. First Alphonse, one of the twins, would pull

the pup's tail ; then came a shriek; then Alfrida, the other, would
tread on a paw—more screams and cries. The washing had to be
hung so high the girl had to stand on a barrel, and if anything hung
an inch too low, those fiends of pups would jump and spring, claw
and tear, until they ruined hundreds of dollars worth of clothes, but
William only smiled and said we made a mighty fuss over a few rags.
After several years of this we moved to a larger city, and what was my
joy to find we only had a small boarded yard to our house. No room
for dogs, thought I ! and for several months we lived in peace, and
the worried look was leaving my eyes, and the few gray hairs, after
. being pulled out, did not return. There was noting too much for me
o do for dear Will. Alas, we were too happy to last. " Rap-it-tap"
came the postman one day, with a letter for Will. Had I known what it
contained, it would have been reduced to ashes before the seal was
broken. But I did not know, so handed it, with a smile, to Will. In
a moment he said "It's from brother Harry. He has a splendid pup !"
—I almost shrieked—" he wants us to keep it for him as he has no
room, being a bachelor."

"But, Will, dear, the yard is too small—"

"Oh, he'll only want us to keep him for a short time."

Arguments, tears, prayers, were of no use. With the daylight came
the pup—now two pups, one for Will, he being so kind! If ever a
poor woman's life was miserable, mine was, for the mischief of all the
pups we ever owned seemed concentrated in these wretched two.

The girl said she would not stay to clean after no dogs, and it was
only by raising her wages and a great deal of coaxing that she did.
Nothing could be hung on the line without a guard to watch the dogs,
and if the attention was one moment diverted, one to ten dollars
worth of damage was done.

One day I was particularly angry; the dogs had destroyed about
thirty-five dollars worth of clothes, embroidered flannels, and the girl's

shawl—she made it lively for Will that night—but he bought her a new shawl and gave me fifty dollars, and smiled and said for us to talk no more about it.

In the morning he told me he was going on a business trip, and to have a couple of clean shirts ready. Oh! here was my opportunity, so selecting the raggedest two I could find, they were soon on the line, but after swinging half the day—without a guard—they were not touched by the dogs! I was not to be baffled thus, so sending for a friend, a perfect adept at mischief, I asked her what was to be done, and the result was, we silently stole to the yard, with scissors in our hands, and snipped and tore those shirts and dragged them in the muddy yard, till they were unrecognizable as masculine garments; then we let the girl into the plot, and returned to await the result. Will was lively and chatty at dinner, and Fanny, my friend, was full of smiles. At last desert was brought in and with the pie and apples came Bridget. "Look at yer shirt Mr. Jones, torn to bits and as black as the chimbly, and its not myself that can wash ye any more, for the mor'n', and drat all dogs and pups, say I."

Will looked grave, but we laughed till the tears came.

"I don't see anything so terribly funny in loosing the shirts," Will remonstrated?

"No, not so funny as forty or fifty dollars worth of flannels in a single day."

He got up from the table in a bad temper, and after a little while said he would have to go down town to purchase some shirts—then calling me aside he said he guessed as I did not like dogs he would take them away. So he did, next morning early. He and father carried the poor things tied in a sack, and left them near a slaughterhouse, so that when found, they could get plenty to eat; and from that day to this our house has been free from dogs." I laughed heartily at her woman's wit and thought perhaps some of my poor worried lady friends could utilize Marian's experience in getting rid of some of their innumerable troubles.

"It's well you did not tell your husband, or he would have swarmed the house with dogs in revenge for being sold !

"So I thought, and that is why I kept my mouth shut," and I admired her discretion.   HOP-O-MY-THUMB.

And this is Marian's secret.

ABOUT GOING ON THE STAGE.

The other morning, Annie, my latest female confidante, tripped into my office, and after the usual salutations were over, she began:

" Mr. ———," as yet she was not so well acquainted as to call me uncle, "a friend of mine wishes to go on the stage, and I came to ask your advice as the only one among my acquaintances who would be likely to have an intelligent opinion on the subject ?"

' Well my dear Mrs. Smith "—she was married although quite young—" I have no personal experience on the subject, but many of my professional friends have told me their trials and triumphs, and some of the petty annoyances connected with that envied life."

"But what do you think of the advisability of adopting it as a profession? A bread profession, I mean."

"My dear, there are many things to take into consideration, which are applicable according to the individual. Do you wish to know if it is advisable for your friend to go on the stage, or for any one in general ?"

"Oh, for my friend of course. You see she's very poor."

"Ah! that is bad, for no one who is very poor, can use that inde-

pendence of action, that is necessary to success; poverty, too, has a de-
pressing effect, causing one to think more meanly of one's self, than
they would dressed fashionably, with a full purse in their pocket—and
causing the public to, also, as for the matter of that!"

"Oh! my, and she has two or three little children, and needs the
money so bad!"

"Worse again, it is a late day to begin such a profession, when a
woman is married and has several children, for no matter how much
genius she has, her children must be her first thought, if she has any
heart; then, too, she is obliged to be off the stage so much, that the
reputation she makes one year, she loses by her absence the next.
One must keep constantly before the public, in one city or another,
I don't believe in remaining always in one place, with their names
often in the papers, or they will be soon forgotten."

"Then you don't believe in a married woman going on the stage?
I thought as there were so many distressed mothers depicted, that a
married woman would have quite an advantage."

"So she would, if she were wealthy enough to have the very best of
servants and nurses, and her mother or sister to oversee them. Now,
I'm not one of those who believe that if an actress has not all the
young fellows in their teens crazy about her, that she is not a success;
for one who is a favorite with the ladies has a still greater chance of
drawing, and they don't care if they are married or single, in fact, I
think they would rather they were married."

"Do you not think it is the easiest way for a woman to make a
living?"

"Do you remember the old recipe of how to cook a hare—'first
catch your hare!'"

"How? I do not understand."

"First, get upon the stage. How many professional people, some
with a great deal of talent, too, do you suppose, are constantly idle, in

every city ?   It is no easy matter to get an engagement of any kind.
Why, some of my acquaintances who have been on the stage for years
are still in the ballet, with a very occasional speaking part, and there
they may remain for years longer unless some lucky *accident* pushes
them forward, for a manager rarely does.   Indeed, I have known
some managers who would keep a person back all they could; and it
is only by the greatest perseverance and energy and confidence in one's
self—mind me, not a foolish self-conceit—for that disgusts—that a
woman makes the least headway.   I think a man has a better chance,
as there are always so many more male characters in the generality of
pieces."

"Why, I thought a manager was glad to get a *debutante* "

"Yes, when the houses are empty, and she will put down her little
seven or eight hundred dollars, and then sometimes the dead, dead
failure the said *debutante* makes, hurts the reputation of the theatre
more than the money she pays helps it.   How many of the ladies,
especially those who made their debut with a little family already on
their hands, are now upon the stage ?   Why, here in our own beautiful city, I can remember, within the year, the first appearance of, I
think, a half-a-dozen Mrs. So-and-So's, who are never heard of, except one, and she made the deadest failure of all, and never will suc-
ceed, as she is *passé* and has not even talent, let alone genius, which
is necessary for a complete success; but she, I presume, has given it
up, as a not paying occupation—at least for her."

"Why, I thought it was so easy.   I have often fancied I could do
as well, or even better than lots of the ladies I see at our best theatres."

I laughed heartily.   "Ah! that's what so many think till they try.
Why, I saw a lady, who brought bills from Australia, with her name as
Lady Macbeth in big letters, fail entirely on the stage of a metropoli-
tan theatre, in only a small part, back up the stage as if she wanted
to go through the scenery, with no word audible except the sentence,

'I'd slap his face!' The next night she did not appear, although her name was on the bills."

"Oh! you discourage me about my friend, for I don't think she had much talent, and I know she has no money; but I thought she could do well enough, and fifty or seventy-five dollars a week would keep her nicely."

"Why, my dear, you must think the theatres are perfect gold mines! Do you know what ballet girls used to get in one of the big western cities? Three dollars a week and dress themselves. That would be scarcely enough to keep a family of several persons."

"Oh!—that is horrid. Why the mean, stingy things."

"Yes, and even then they were overrun with applications, just because so many think as you do, that it is so easy, that one can step into a great profession, begin at the top, with a month or two of indifferent preparation and shine as stars! many who attempt it had better be at the wash tub, or sewing machine, or making good bread, something they could do with credit to themselves and pleasure to their fellow beings."

If one must go upon the stage, if their love for it is so great they are ready to endure any hardships and privations, besides any amoun of snubbing and criticisim by the papers; if they are willing to give their whole heart and mind to their profession; if their head is so strong that no amount of flattery or temptation is able to turn it; if they can live for years without fancying they are in love; if they have immense genius and some beauty and are still young, then I say go."

"Keep a clear head, a free heart, and mount the ladder of Fame as rapidly as possible. Make the most of your youth, and heaven bless and protect you in one of the noblest of professions."

My friend sighed and said :

" Well! I'll tell her what you say, but she'll be so disappointed."

" She had better be so now, than afterwards."

" That's true." And Annie sorrowfully left the office.

Hop-o'-My-Thumb.

SPEAK YOUR MIND.

Speak your mind; speak it right out; show your independence; it's manly, too.   If you think Mr. — is a villian, say so; or if your private opinion is that he is not overburthened with sense call him a blanked fool on the public streets; it will show your courage, and that you're not afraid of him.   If you hear a party of gentlemen whom you know, or are slightly acquainted with, discussing some topic, just step up and speak your mind on the subject without waiting to asked; it will show that you consider yourself just as good as any of them.

If you know anything to the detriment of a public man, or one in high position, tell it to every one you meet; it will strengthen their good opinion of you, and help to destroy their faith in him, and so conduce to the equalizing of the race.   And if you know anything against a woman, speak your mind, or a little more so; your gentlemen fiiends will think you are a "knowing dog," and the ladies be fascinated by your Don Juan experiences.

There's nothing like it.   If you think a bank is a little shaky, rush and get your money out, then tell every body the bank is going to burst; you'll most likely cause a "run" on it, and make your words come true; no matter how many widows and orphans are left to starve by your frankness, or how many an honest man to die of grief, you're all right; you've got your money, and spoken your mind.   If you hear that Mr. So-and-So isn't square in his dealings, no matter how worthless a man informs you that that is his opinion, tell every one that he is a thief and cheats his customers; gives short weight, and adulterates his goods, or keeps the very poorest; you'll soon injure his business, no matter if he is a good man, entirely unknown to you, and never did you the least harm. You have performed your duty to society, for you heard so, and are therefore blamless of the consequences.

And if some miserable scamp brags of his success with some respectable girl, no matter if it's ever so much a lie, stare at her when ever you see her in the street; it won't hurt if you even wink at her Point her out to all your acquaintances as So-and-So's girl, no matter if it blasts her reputation, and your gentlemen friends forbid their daughters associating with her; and seeing she is avoided by her own sex, she finally goes to destruction, and perhaps fills a suicide's grave. What should you care ? You heard so, and only spoke your mind.

Why, it is something to brag of, this frankness! Witness the man who says:

"I always speak my mind, I do; there's no foolishness about me!" He is so well liked by those who know him, and he is too frank to be polite.

"It's only hypocrisy to bow and smile at a man when you don't care for him, and hoping he's well when you don't hope anything about it; and as for giving your seat to a woman in the cars, I'll be hanged if I ever do. Why can't a man be frank and do only what he feels like doing ?" This is the catechism he acts by, and when he dies, how he is bemoaned and wept for!

And aren't clubs splendid places to speak your minds ? No matter on what a slight thread of truth some wicked story is based, tell it over and over again, and give your opinion besides; this dresses it—gives it color, and when it leaves the clubs you wouldn't know your own story; no matter what home it makes desolate, the story is too good to keep. Oh! what a precious set of old gossips you club men are!

The ladies never, or hardly ever, speak their minds. They don't like sewing circles where they can do a few stitches for the poor, while politely killing some woman's reputation with all the sweetness possible, forgetting they are mothers themselves, with daughters whose reputations are as dear to them as their heart's blood, yet neglecting to spare the blighting word for some body else's loved daughters. Oh, no; they are so reticent about all the evil they hear, that they never repeat it at morning calls, and not remembering the exact words never give it in language of their own, which don't detract from the point of scandal, you may be sure! Oh, no!

One single case. Oh! yes; two, happen every day in this goodly city, where the women courageously say just what they think.

"You nasty, mean, stingy thing, you! Can't you come home and cut the wood, and not be here every day playing the dirty cards? Oh, you're a nice set, enticing a husband from his home to play cards for the mean whisky you love to drink, you mean, dirty dog, you!" Now, that's a brave woman. All the gentlemen assembled in that sample room think her a fine specimen of womanhood, and wonder how in the world a husband could ever leave her side! How much better this is than merely to appear at the door and say:

"Mr. Jones!" and have the aforesaid Jones spring up as if he had sat on a pin, and throwing down his half finished hand, walk off dignified with his dignified wife. Now that spoils all sport, and the rest of the men have nothing to joke him about. But even that is more emphatic and expressive than the timid—

"Pet, dinner is ready," whispered at the door. Men don't appreciate that, and come when they want, no matter if the other Pet is waiting and dinner does get cold. It is so much better to speak out and act out your mind. Just walk in and take him by the ear with a grip like a pair of dentist's nippers, so that either he or the ear has to come, and say gently:

"Love, dinner is on the table!" You speak your mind, and the gentlemen think he at least has a treasure who knows her business, and won't stand any nonsense. They know that ends it, and he gets no Caudle lecture.

Oh! gentlemen, oh! ladies, speak your minds on every subject, and on all occasions. Don't you believe that any one was ever scandalized into an early grave; don't trouble yourself that your words ever helped cause the waters to close over one more unfortunate, or the bullet to go crashing through a brain, sending the soul, all unprepared to its Maker.

Don't you believe that the charity which covers a multitude of sins, without which all goodness is as sounding brass; don't you believe that it means to think kindly of one another; to speak only the good you know; to try to cover our brother's fault from the gaping eyes and ears of curiosity; don't you believe it is to guard the reputation of the helpless, to stimulate the weak or erring, to regain the lost path. Don't you believe that Christ's Divine Charity is so often the Charity of Silence?   Hop-o-My-Thumb.

Susie's idea.

ALL FOR LOVE.

Chapter I.

It is midnight in Lady Elmer Dudley's boudoir, the air is filled with a subtle perfume that clings to laces, curtains, statues, flowers; it feels the abode of passionate, dreamy luxury. The presence of a pert and pretty lady's maid slightly destroys the fascination. She is looking in the mirror with a pleased satisfaction on her face. These were her thoughts, for few people talk alone, save in plays or when they get old and witchish.

" It's fine feathers makes fine birds, say I. Who wouldn't look well with a long train, and hair all be-jimcracked up with diamants and things? I should like to mingle in yonder gay and festive scene, and try the power of my charms among my equals." Then as the music came softly and sweetly from the ball-room, she became enthusiastic : Now there's the divine polka. Oh ! for a partner." But no one was there, so she seized one of the gilded chairs. " What! lovely woman reduced to this ! A stick; but what are men but sticks—sometimes, or why would they say "she picked up a crooked stick at last." Then she laughed, overflowing with a natural vivacity of spirits, and danced around the room with the little chair as partner. A low knock at the door caused her to stop, making a pretty picture.

A voice outside said in a loud whisper:

"May I come in ?" It was Cubby, Sir Francis Hilton's valet, who was a guest in the ball-room beyond.

"Oh, there's my young man !"

"The highflyers are all polkaing; can I speak a word to my charmer ?"

" 'Sh! one short moment, Cubby!" She opens the door wider, he takes her round the waist, and they polka extravagantly till she is out of breath and falls into a chair. He goes to the bureau, and examining the beautiful things there, says :

"Oh! this is an earthly Paradise! What is this ? Cologney ?" And he hands the exquisite perfume bottle to the pretty Willet, and tells her "Fumigate me, my charmer;" and bending his head, she saturates his hair; then he pulls out an immense lace handkerchief, which she treats in the same manner.

"That will do. It's nice to be a gentleman's gentleman; don't you think so, Willet ?"

"It's nicer to be a lady's lady, don't you think so, Cubby ?"

"Pon honor, couldn't tell, never being a female, you know. Ah, the polka is ended; I must make myself scarce—but I should like to see the beauties in all their flustration from the dance."

"You indiscreet man ! it would be as much as my place is worth. They are coming—vanish !"

" I vanish!" and he does. She throws herself in a chair using her apron as a fan. " I declare, I'm all in a flutter! If they had seen him here, what would they have thought ? Oh, my!" she stood up meekly as two beautiful women entered, Lady Clare De Mille, blonde, medium height and gentle, with a reserve force beneath the surface; and Lady Elmer Dudley, brunette, tall and passionate, both dressed in the extreme of wealth and fashion. Elmer was looking at her friend, pleased, yet half amazed; she said:

"Oh! Clare, you look beautiful to-night! Not the splendor that dazzles and repels, but the beauty that attracts and subdues."

" Elmer, don't spoil your little friend. Flattery from a woman is more subtle and dangerous than the little civilities we have a right to expect from our cavaliers."

" Then how you dance! Your very heart seems in it. The electricity of your happiness is sensibly affecting every one in yonder ball room. Clare, tell me the secret."

" Would you know what renders earth a Paradise to me to-night ? Then I will tell you; the most potent of all powers—love."

Willet, standing behind them, clasps her hands in feminine approval and delight, uttering a subdued " oh, my!"

" Is it the most potent ?" Elmer asked, with an accent that showed she thought otherwise.

" What else could change a desert into an Eden, a prison into a palace? What other power would make us willing to harden our dainty hands, or brown our snow-white brows ? Let misfortune come to lovers truly wedded, what will they not endure ? hardships, trials, or even death, before a separation."

"I should not wish you for a rival, Clare ; that earnestness and enthusiasm would keep a lover true and firm. But there is a feeling more powerful even than love—jealousy ! Clare, as much as I love you, did you come between me and my heart's idol, I would kill you." But the gentle Clare only laughed. "Oh, Elmer, never fear, my love is too constant to change, and my heart is so filled with one image there is not room for any other !"

"That is my dear, true friend," and she kissed her, gaily. "Neither shall my heart wander from my chosen one, so we shall each be as secure in our love as a queen on her throne." They were interrupted by Cubby bringing in a tray of refreshments. He handed it to them.

"Sherbet or ices, ladies?" Elmer, smiling, turned to Clare, and said :

"A little refreshment, Clare, dear, will enable us better to go through with our arduous task. This dancing, dancing, till even the stars are weary and hiding their paling splendor, is no easy task, fair ladye mine !" So they sit, Clare taking an ice, and Elmer Sherbet. But the music begins, and Clare is impatient to go back into the ball room. "It is almost impossible to sit calmly sipping this prosaic ice, while the music of the divine Mozart makes my very nerves thrill !"

" Do you never tire !"

"Not when my heart's chosen whispers words of love that are audible to no ears but mine, and his arm encircles me. Elmer, I have never waltzed before save with my brother, so to-night I have tasted for the first time the delirium of the waltz."

"My idol has not so honored me as yet, but then we are still un-betrothed."

"Then you have yet to know earth's sweetest pleasure. What woman would not envy me the love of Sir Francis Hilton?"

Lady Elmer started voilently, and the glass fell from her hand, breaking to pieces. The servants sweep them up, and leave the room. Poor Clare was frightened, and springing to her side, asked:

" What is it, Elmer ? Are you in pain ?"

"Yes; a deathly pain at my heart; it will be over soon." Then looking in the glass, she said: " How pale it has made me!" Clare handed her some perfume, and wished to call Willet, but Elmer shook her head.

" What silly girls we are," she said smilling. " See, my color is returning; I shall be ready for the Lancers;" and as Willet entered, she bade her re-arrange the flowers in her hair.

" Now who is beautiful?" cried Clare. " The color of your cheek rivals the fairest rose, and your eyes flash brighter than the diamonds on your brow."

"Would that my chosen had thought so," she said sadly; then suddenly changing: " Are not these beautiful ? My dear father gave them to me on this, my birthnight;" and she took from her ears two of the largest and most brilliant of diamonds and handed them to Clare.

"Yes, they are very beautiful, and see ! they sparkle as brightly as if you had not suffered that dreadful pain just now; so you are in no danger while your diamonds shine."

"Were the legend true, my diamonds would be as lead—but do not let us talk nonsense. See how my diamonds sparkle for you!" and she put them in Clare's ears. "So no ill omen warns you to-night. Look, do they not become you ?"

"They are finer than any I possess. Diamonds have a beauty of their own, without any regard to their intrinsic value."

Elmer sends Willet for a glass of water, then perfumes Clare's handkerchief that she lays down while she removes the earrings from her ears.

"I expect Sir Francis is wondering what has become of us," said Clare, looking toward the door.

An expression of pain and horror passed over Elmer's face, as she pushed Clare's handkerchief toward her. Willet entered with the water, and Cubby came in haste, saying:

"They are asking for the ladies."

Elmer suddenly put her hands to her ears, then looked on the bureau, exclaiming:

"Where are my earrings? Cubby, call a policeman quick! I have been robbed!"

Cubby went to the door and blew his policeman's whistle, and then returned; but Willett was indignant: "You need not try to put the theft on me, mem; I left the room with them hanging in Lady Clare's ears." Cubby quietly felt his hair, hoping his charmer didn't pour them on his head with the "Cologney." But the policeman arrived, and asked Lady Elmer what she wished.

"My diamond earrings cannot be found. They are my dear father's gift, and I would not lose them for fifty times their value." Hearing the policeman's whistle, and the excitement, Sir Francis Hilton and many of the guests, with Clare's mother and Elmer's father, came to see what had happened. The policeman walked directly over to Willet, and laid his hand upon her shoulder.

"Come, my girl, what have you got to say for yourself?" But Willet knowing her innocence, and having plenty of spirit, took his hand from her shoulder, and dusted her dress with a lace handkerchief.

"Hands off, if you please, Mr. Policeman, you are on the wrong track. You will have to hunt higher game to-night!" she said significantly, and Cubby shook his fist at him, but behind his back.

"Dear Elmer, they were here a few moments ago; they cannot have been stolen!" and Clare looked eagerly on floor and bureau.

"See, they are nowhere to be found;" then in a stern voice she said: "Willet, what have you done with them ?"

This made her very angry, and she replied in a high excited voice: "You can't lay it on me, my lady. I left the room with them sticking in Lady Clare's ears, and she admiring herself in the looking-glass, and I hadn't reached my lady with the water she ordered, before she discovered she were robbed. Oh! if you want to see, here is my pockets!" and she turned them inside out, throwing on the floor various articles; a love letter, several shillings, a piece of cake and an apple, that she had just taken to refresh herself. "Are you satisfied, Mr. Policeman? Cubby turned his pockets out, too, and the other servants crowded both the doors. Then Elmer said with a start:

"Oh, I remember; my friend, Lady Clare and I, were alone—of course they can be found. Policeman, your services are not needed."

"You sent for me, my lady, and my duty is to arrest the thief, if you have been robbed. Her ladyship being innocent, will not object to being searched. It is a mere formality."

"I decline to be searched!" Clare replied with great dignity. They all looked astonished. "I am an Earl's daughter, descended from a line of ancestors, whose proud boast has been for five hundred years, their escutcheon without a soil!" Sir Francis stepped to her side and said:

"The lady is right; she shall not be searched."

Elmer turned to the policeman:

"Officer, please go; you see, we have no use for you."

But he would not stir.

" If the lady declines to give proof of her innocence the only duty left me will be to arrest her.!"

But they all exclaimed in horror, " Oh!" and Sir Francis said coldly and determined:

" Do not dare!"

"Officer, please go. I would rather lose my fortune, than my friend should suffer such an indignity."

"Lay your hand on that lady, and you are a dead man!" But Clare spoke sweetly:

"Sir Francis, it needs no blood to vindicate my innocence; Heaven will do that!" and she took her hand from her pocket, holding her little lace handkerchief, and pointed upward.

But what were those sparks of light that fell from the upraised hand? The Policeman pointed in triumph to the floor: "See the diamonds!"

Sir Francis prayed, "Heaven shield her!" And Elmer burst into tears, and cried, "Oh, my friend!"

But Clare still stood, with her hand yet raised, a statue of innocence.

Chapter II.

The whole house was in confusion. Of course every one had their opinion, even to the servants, whether the Lady Clare was guilty or not guilty. Willet ran hither and thither, helping the guests, who were as hurried in their departure as if a pestilence had struck the house. But who can blame them? Sorrow and misfortune are so hard to witness; we know not what to say, or how to act, and if we are prompted to console, are very like to utter words we may long wish unsaid. The tongue is a terrible little mischief maker, sometimes, too, when we think it covered with the balm of peace. Willet had lost all her gaiety. "Ah!" she thought, "Fine feathers don't always make fine birds, it seems." In her heart, she was sorry for Clare, and thought the diamonds must have gotten into her pocket without her knowledge—perhaps caught in her handkerchief, or fallen in. Then she uttered aloud:

"How quickly our fine ball has broken up. Why, some of the

ladies even fainted, and some said they were never so insulted in all their lives. The heartless things!'' But Cubby stopped any further soliloquism by throwing his arms around her in a consoling manner, and said in a pathetic voice:

'' Dear Willet, I'm so glad you turned your pockets out, and didn't pour the diamonds on me with the perfumery; for how could such a gentle being as me, bear even the suspicin of such a dreadful thing? To think that our grand birthnight ball should end with such a catastrophe. Well, all is vanity!''

"There's a mystery about them diamants that I don't like. When's the trial to be?''

"As soon as possible. My lady's out on bail, but wants her honorable name cleared. Ah! she should not have let vanity get the better of her.''

' 'What! do you suppose she stole them?''

'' Of course; how else could they have got into her ladyship's pocket?''

"And do you suppose a lady would descend to such a thing ?''

"Why not? They say you women folks would sell your souls almost, for a bit of finery.''

'' They say! May I ask your highness who 'they' are?''

"Mankind, the people, we, the world!''

'' Oh! we! then 'we' had better look into our pockets, and see if hat gorgeous handkerchief 'we' displayed last night hasn't transferred itself into mine!''

"My charming Willet, I only wish it had, and me with it!''

"Then let me tell you, Mr. Cubby, my pockets would be shook into the dust bin, as soon as my feet could carry me there!'' and she flounced out of the room as only an indignant woman can.

But Cubby only whistled, and thought what a tartar she was, when Sir Francis entered the room, and told him to order Lady De Mille's carriage immediately.   He felt so bitterly outraged and insulted that his betrothed wife should have suffered such an indignity, and in the house, too, of the lady who had always appeared to be such a dear friend.   He suspected some plot, but what could be the motive?   He could not even conceive of one.

He determined that he would plead her cause; knowing and feeling her innocence as he did, he thought it would be easy to place the jury *en rapport* with himself, and so cause her speedy vindication.

Clare's mother was nearly frantic, and rushing to Sir Francis, begged him to save her innocent child, that the trial she knew would kill her.

"We should take an example from Lady Clare herself, who is so conscious of her own innocence that she does not shed a tear.   Did you know that Lady Elmer offered to go her bail for twenty thousand pounds?"

"Do not speak of that heartless woman!   What wrong have we done her that she should throw such a terrible suspicion on my darling child?"

"It was all done in the excitement of the moment.   Surely no woman in her heart could so wish to injure another."

"Ah, Sir Francis, you do not know women yet as I do.   I have lived in this world sixty-five years, and I tell you, the fury of wild beasts, the terror of the tempest, the anger of man, are pleasant experiences to the demoniac passion of a jealous woman."

Sir Francis knew this could not possibly be the motive, as he had hardly spoken to the Lady Elmer.   But Cubby announced the carriage before he could reply.

Lady Elmer brought Clare to her mother.   She had been uttering phrases of consolation, but Clare had replied never a word.

Sir Francis pressed her hand tenderly, as he helped her into the carriage; the pressure spoke sympathy, love, and belief in her inno-cence.   So Clare went home almost happy, thinking that the morrow would clear up the mystery, and all would be bright again.

Chapter III.

What is so impressive as an English court of justice? The scarlet and black robes, the ermine, the wigs, the dim light, the silence, broken only by the necessities of the trial; no flippant lawyer insulting witnesses, to show to the world his wit; no ink-bottle throwing, or cane-thrashing as occur sometimes in enlightened, deliberative bodies. All is solemnity. Once seen, it is a picture never to be forgotten.

The massive stone building, with the ever memorable name, the street itself, calling up so many legends of the past. Romantic, melancholy, blood-stirring, all are conducive to inspire awe as you approach, and to lower your voice to a solemn monotone, as you enter the heavy doorway.

Here in an ante-room, waiting for the verdict, were many relations and servants of the two families, and nervous friends who would faint at sight of all the paraphernalia of stern justice. Some were speaking in little groups in whispers, some sat with hands folded, and dreamy eyes gazing into vacancy.

But the quiet was suddenly disturbed by the door violently opening, and Lady Ashley Downington entering in a rage followed by Jonquel carrying her inseparable poodle, and Lord Butterfly bringing up the rear.

"To think that I should be treated so! What is the use of our Magna Charta, if our personal liberty is to be so interfered with? Where I go, Master Pinkette goes, or I'll find out the meaning o British liberty."

"Yeth, yeth, ith too bad. I would appeal to her Gracious Majesty.'

"What harm did the dear little innocent darling do? I'm sure they ought to be pleased with his presence as a contrast where there's so much guilt."

"Yeth, yeth; that's what I thay!" and Lord Butterfly laughed in a way we should call—well, rather idiotic.

"He did not bark even, but was watching proceedings with more interest than half the bipeds there, if he is a quadruped."

"Yeth, yeth; he—he looked quite withe!" and he laughed again.

"The Barbarians! To think we should suffer the indignity of—well, to put it in the politest terms possible, the effect is the same—we are turned out."

"Yeth, so it seems;" and he consoled her with the peculiar laugh.

The ladies all said it was too bad, and petted and caressed Pinkette till he looked sour. For quite a time he was the centre of interest, and the trial was forgotten. Each lady that owned a canine pet, told each other lady of its pains and troubles and its dear cunning little tricks; and several fast friendships were made then and there, by revelations of mutual sympathy. And Lady Downington added two more names to her visiting list for the same reason.

After the subject was fully exhausted, they suddenly became interested in the proceedings of the trial.

"Was it going against poor Lady Clare?" asked a nervous lady friend?

"Indeed I could not tell. I was so engaged watching my little darling here I had no eyes or ears for aught else."

But we will leave these people of petty hearts and brains, whose lives are made up of twaddle and dogs, whose sluggish blood is only stirred by danger to their pets; who could sympathize with the stomach-ache of a poodle, forgetting that the hopes of a human life were being shattered, and that a mother's heart was suffering the intense agony a mother alone can feel.

In the court Lady Clare, pale as death, stood in the prisoner's box, her mother as near her as allowed; but, oh, how changed! Her gray ringlets of one short week ago, were now as white as snow, and the lines about her face had deepened as if by years of sorrow.

Lady Elmer, with a face almost as pale as Clare's, listened with an intense eagerness to every word.

The clerk called in that peculiar voice:

"Prisoner at the bar, do you plead guilty or not guilty?"

Clare stood up and replied in a low voice, but so intense that every one could hear—yes, and feel too.

"Not guilty!"

"Policeman No. 5!" called the clerk, and as he entered the box the Queen's counsel began his questioning.

"On the night of the 3d of June, were you called to the house of Lord Charles Lucius Dudley in your official capacity?"

"I was."

"For what purpose were you called?"

"Lady Elmer Dudley complained of being robbed; I was called to detect and arrest the thief."

"What persons were present at the time?"

"Lady Elmer Dudley, the prisoner, Sarah Willet and Alphonse Cubby."

"Whom did Lady Elmer Dudley suspect of the robbery?"

"She addressed to her maid, Sarah Willet, these words: 'Willet, what have you done with them?"

Willet could not sit quiet and hear this imputation on her character before so many people, so jumping up she said quickly:

"But I had never laid my fingers on them, my lord."

"Silence in the court!"

"Were the actions of Sarah Willet suspicious?" continued the counsel.

"Not at all, my lord; she turned her pockets inside out, and seemed willing and anxious to prove her innocence."

"That will do."

"Lady Elmer Dudley!" called the clerk. And all eyes were turned on the beautiful lady, who seemed to suffer for her friend more than she did for herself.

"On the night of June the 3d you lost some valuable diamonds; whom did you suspect of the theft?"

"My lord—"

"Please answer the court direct."

"Lady Clare De Mille and myself alone were present," and she hung her head as if in deep grief.

"Had the prisoner expressed any admiration of them previously, or showed in any way that she coveted them ?"

"She had remarked about my diamonds sparkling so brightly, that I tried them in her ears; looking at herself in the glass, she said, 'they are finer than any I possess.' "

"When did you miss them ?"

"A few moments afterward, when we were about to return to the ball room."

"That will do, your ladyship." And Elmer bowed and returned to her place, the picture of a witness who had unwillingly given pain to a dear friend.

Again the policeman was called.

"Did the prisoner appear willing to be searched?"

"She declined, saying she was an Earl's daughter."

"My lord, my daughter had a letter in her pocket, she did not wish made public; it was a proposal of—"

"Silence in the court!"

"Oh, my lord, let me speak for my child; she is my only daughter, and I know how good she is."

The poor mother burst into an agony of tears, but calmed the exhibition of her grief, on being told very kindly and gently by an officer sent by the Judge, that she must not speak in court unless she was questioned.

"What else occured on the night aforesaid?"

"Lady Elmer Dudley seemed most anxious that I should leave the house remembering that the prisoner and herself alone were present. Sir Francis Hilton threatened me with personal violence should I perform my duty, but the prisoner calling on Heaven to witness her innocence, without thinking, pulled her handkerchief from her pocket, and the diamonds fell on the floor!" There was a sensation in the court, but Willet jumped up again, saying emphatically:

"But I don't believe she put them there."

"Silence in the court!" and the irrepressible Willet sat down with a jerk. Sir Francis Hilton was called as the next witness, and it was a study to watch the faces of Clare and Elmer, as he gave his testimony After several questions he was asked if he had witnessed the falling of the diamonds from the prisoner's handkerchief.

"I did, but believe they came there by accident."

"We wish facts, and not opinions. What is your knowledge of the character of the prisoner at the bar? Has it always stood well, previously, for honesty?"

"I will cross swords with you, my lord, for this insult!" He grasped the hilt of his sword, but poor Clare cried out:

"Oh, Sir Francis, speak for me ; tell them you have known me since a little child, and that I never, in thought, word, or deed, broke the holy eighth commandment!" Many eyes were wet with tears, and many hearts felt pity for the beautiful, pale Lady Clare. The Judge asked the Queen's counsel if he had any more witnesses to call.

"None, my lord!" But Cubby was quite disappointed at not having the notoriety of being a witness in this case, and muttered *sotto voce:*

"They don't ask me anything!" The Judge then said:

"The case for the prosecution is then closed. Counsel for the prisoner."

Elmer arose in agitation, and asked in a seemingly imploring voice:

" My Lord, may I not speak for my friend ?" But the Judge shook his head, and Sir Francis arose and commenced his argument.

"My lord, and gentlemen, it is with intense pain that I see so estimable a lady injured by the least breath of such a foul suspicion. For those who know her, she needs no defence. Her blameless life, her filial love, her divine charity, give a verdict in her favor that the opinion of no jury in England could outweigh. It is true the circumstances of the case appear against her, but let us pause and observe the picture. Two ladies—friends—retire for a few moments to rest after the fatigue of the dance; with girlish playfulness they admire each other's jewelry, seeing if this or that is becoming to them ; they are standing by the dressing table ; the earrings are placed in dainty ears by loving fingers ; being duly admired, the fleecy handkerchief is laid upon the table while the earrings are withdrawn, and for the moment quite forgotten. What more natural than that the slender golden wires should catch in the meshes of the lace, and they should find themselves where their presence would condemn as guilty the most innocent of women ? Their owner, in the first anguish of their fancied loss, exclaiming she is robbed !

" Now let us reason why the prisoner should not commit the theft of which she is accused. First, had she desired an exact counterpart of the earrings belonging to her friend, she had only to mention her wish to an indulgent mother ; then the lady herself is singularly free from the little vanities of her sex. Would she soil the escutcheon that, since the founding of the family, has been unsullied, for the gratification of a mere whim ?

" Brought up by a conscientious mother, she has been taught what is due to Heaven and man. Would she then violate every right of sacred hospitality for a mere bauble? Look at the lady herself, the picture of innocence, grieved to the heart at an unjust accusation ! Look at the mother, bowed down with anguish that none but a mother can know ! What can compensate her for her sufferings ? Not even the hope, nay, the certainty of the speedy relief of the daughter so loved, so prayed for ! My lord, and gentlemen of the jury, I rest the case on its merits alone, beseeching you to relieve the anguish of the mother and the humiliation of the daguhter, as quickly as human justice will permit you." Again that sensation in court like a gentle breeze passing through a grove on a Summer day.

The Queen's counsel arose :

" My lord, and gentlemen of the jury !" Then dropping the deferential tone, a slight smile lit up his face and a tinge of sarcasm, like a thread, was interwoven with his words. " My learned friend has depicted, with great pathos, the sufferings of an innocent victim ! Let us turn to the evidence ; that must be our guide to justice.

" Not being intimately acquainted with the prisoner, I cannot affirm from personal knowledge, as my learned brother does, that she is singularly free from the vanities of her sex. Turning to the evidence, we find that the looking glass was the same to her as to the rest of Eve's daughters ; that she admired trinkets and possessed them, and in her own words the diamonds of her friend were finer than any she possessed ; that, my lord, is the key to the whole transaction.

" Do we not know that even a king cannot brook a rival monarch's possessing finer jewels than himself ?

"The refusal to be searched—the flimsy excuse of the letter, the jewels found secreted on her person, is *prima facie* evidence of her guilt. Does the case stand so isolated and alone in English jurisprudence that it has no counterpart ? Does a title and a fortune prevent crime ! Alas, our records say no !

" What is it, then, so calls for sympathy in the prisoner's case ? Had it been one of the people, no noble lord would have volunteered his maiden effort in her defence ; had it been one of the people—one of the lower class, and instead of diamonds to adorn her person, it had been bread to fill a starving mouth, how soon would the floor of a prison be her resting place, and the rats and spiders her companions? And shall this prisoner go free because her dress is silk and her face is fair, when neither want nor poverty tempted her ; only the covetuousness of a vain heart?

"Do not let justice change its name to condemnation for the half starved poor, and acquittal for the guilty rich ! I, too, my lord, rest the case on its merits !"

Clare looked like one stupified, but a strange gleam shone in Elmer's eyes. The judge then rose and gave his charge to the jury.

"Gentlemen of the jury, we are here as Heaven's ministers of justice! Compassion, pity, personal consideration, must not influence your decision. Were we only disciples of the of Goddess Pity, a woman's tears, a mother's prayers, would outweigh all other considerations; but stern justice must be blind to all the gentle emotions.

"If the evidence in the case points to the prisoner as innocent, your verdict must be acquittal, or if there is even a doubt in your minds, the verdict must be for acquittal. But if you believe, and agree, that the accused did purposely and feloniously secrete the diamonds, your verdict must be for condemnation!" Then there was a slight buzz all over the court, then silence.

The jury consulted together without leaving their box. Clare seemed to listen with her eyes. After a pause of intense anxiety, the foreman arose and delivered the verdict:

"We, the jury, after carefully considering the evidence of the case, find the prisoner guilty of the charge in the indictment !"

The De Mille party appeared stunned. The Judge then addressed Clare :

"Prisoner at the bar, stand up. Have you anything to say against the finding of the jury?"

Clare arose, trembling.

"My lord, I am overwhelmed with surprise and confusion, that men who profess to be advocates of Heaven's divine justice, should count as guilty any one, no matter what evidence of innocence their whole life should give, who is only suspected of a crime. Oh, my lord, let my mother's tears speak for me. Have mercy! have mercy! or you will break her heart!" She could say no more, but sank, weeping, into her seat, and the Judge gave sentence.

"Prisoner, the high position you hold, the purity of a long line of ancestors, your wealth, all should have been bars to your committing such a disreputable crime, plunging your family into such deep grief. But vanity and cupidity proved too strong. They have been the cause of more falls from virtue than poverty and hatred combined. As a punishment for your crime and to deter others from following in your steps and sharing your fate, we condemn you to seven years of servitude and exile in the Island of Australia!"

With a shriek, Clare fell senseless to the floor.

Chapter IV.

Six months had passed since Lady Clare had been sent to Australia. No efforts had been spared to obtain her release, but all were unavailing.

Lady Elmer was gayer than ever. She seemed to seek excitement with a feverish eagerness that acquaintances thought heartlessness, but friends considered the strivings of a tender nature to momentarily forget the pain caused by a friend's sufferings—sufferings, too, she had apparently tried so perseveringly to alleviate.

One morning, Willet was clipping the dead leaves from the vines in a hanging basket in the morning room. She was standing on a table with the morning paper under her feet, and she thus gave vent to her thoughts:

"Well, some people can clip, and clip away at their consciences just as I clip these vines, and it don't seem to hurt them a bit—more contrary-wise, they thrive on the treatment, just as these vines do. Six months ago my lady's dearest friend was sent to that dreadful Australia, yet she now lives in a perfect whirligig of pleasure and excitement; but when she comes home at night, or rather in the morning, and throws off her beautiful clothes, she looks so pale and haggard, that my heart really aches for her; and I wonder why she goes out so much if it makes her feel so bad, when her friend's in such sad trouble?" She got down from the table and surveyed her work critically, even if she was thinking of something else.

" Then, too, why does Sir Francis come here so much? 'Tain't as a lover, for he's so cautious like; but my lady's desparately in love with him; she couldn't hide it from a cat!" Then she gaped and looked around for the most comfortable place to take a rest. The room was exquisitely furnished, with all the taste of a passionate, educated woman; furnished, too, to harmonize with her clear, dark beauty, and to form a fitting background for the picture she made when she entered it.

" Heigh-ho!" and she sank down in a crimson satin easy chair, with a great deal of lazy pleasure. " I'm a little 'onweed' myself, with so much gaiety. My lady won't ring for some time, so I'll regale myself with a little intellectual food." So she took the paper and began at the top. "'Bonnets from Paris.' I don't want any. 'Immense sacrifice of dry goods.' Sacrifices ahead, it doesn't interest me. ' Murder of a young lady by her lover.' Ah! that's interesting. What's this just after the murder. ' Departure of Sir Francis Hilton for Ausralia.' Oho! what's up? A rescue I shouldn't wonder. How romantic!" She had her back to the door, with her feet stretched out on an ottoman; she had a small foot and rather liked to look at her pretty slippers; but Lady Elmer had entered, and walking across the room stood in front of her before she noticed her presence, then she jumped up confused and blushing.

" Beg pardon my lady; I did not know you were stirring, but thought as you wouldn't want me for a short time I'd rest a bit and read the news. Look what I saw—' Departure of Sir Francis Hilton for Australia!'"

"Where? Let me see it quick!" and she grasped the paper with an eagerness that did not at all surprise the far-seeing Willet.

" There, next to the interesting murder of a young lady." She motioned for Willet to leave the room. She read the brief announcement and it seemed to rack her very soul.

"What does it mean? Is he going there to release her. Have I sacrificed peace and happiness, and imperiled my soul's salvation, to be as far from the fulfillment of my wishes, as when I was innocent? I must prevent his going, but how? My terrible love has not been rewarded by one kind word, so what influence can I bring to bear sufficiently powerful to compel him to change his determination? What a weak thing is a woman! Weak in a thousand ways, having the will so strong yet powerless to execute."

Here Willet knocked at the half open door, but Elmer not noticing it, she put her head in and said:

"Lady Ashley Downington is in the blue parlor."

"Must I endure that tedious old woman when my brain is on fire to be at work? But Lady Ashley had followed Willet, considering herself a privileged friend, and entered a moment after she was announced as being in the blue parlor. She was old and eccentric, and led her beloved "Pinkette" a rather pretty white poodle, by blue and red ribbons.   In her actions she was a youthful old lady, and talked quite gushingly.

"My dear Elmer, I knew after our conversation last night that you would be as anxious to see me as I am to see you, so I did not wait for ceremony, hoping to catch you in delightful *dishabille*, so that I could tell his lordship that beauty unadorned is adorned the most; really and truly in your case—well, how d'ye do?   You may kiss me on the left cheek, but respect the rouge, dear."

Elmer shook her hand, but scarcely touched her cheek with her lips, she was so annoyed.   Then she asked her to sit down, which she did, taking the dog on her lap.

"I am glad to see you so well, after the gaieties of last night."

"Well?   I was never better in all my life.   I shall outwear a dozen of you young people yet!   And wasn't the ball last night a magnificent success! and the dresses! but your's was the loveliest in the room—so I told Lord Butterfly—you see I call him Butterfly, because he always wears such loves of neckties!   'Butterfly,' said I, 'Look at Lady Elmer Dudley; she is dressed the loveliest and in the most *recherché* taste of any lady in the room.' "

"Indeed you were very complimentary, Lady Downington; I suppose I ought to be grateful."

"Not at all, my dear—you see I want the excitement of a little match-making, and I know of no two people in the United Kingdom, so suited to each other as your sweet ladyship and my Butterfly.   He's a perfect Monte Cristo for wealth! and how you could spend it!   A villa on the Rhine, dear, and every Summer a little *écarté* at that delightful Baden-Baden !   Then, too, the poor fellow is desperately in love.   I boldly accused him of it last night, and he replied, ' Pon honor now ; ah! really !   So you see you have only to smile upon him to be one of the very richest ladies of England."

"Then I am afraid I shall remain Elmer Dudley many years to come."

" Oh! don't! for an old maid with a dozen pet cats is abominable!" Elmer could not help smiling, and pointing to the dog, said :

"Would a dozen King Charles' make it any better?"

"Ah! that is very different! But maiden ladies rarely take to them. By the way, don't you think Pinkette is looking very miserable? Doctor Take-all-De-Tour has been his physician for six months, but if he does not improve shortly under his treatment, I shall really have to send to the Continent for help, or take him there myself. Poor little darling, your eyes look so dull to-day!" and she patted his head; but he whined and barked so that she was frightened. "Listen! I know that he is taken worse!" Then turning to Willet, she said: My good girl, won't you call my footman?"

"Yes, my lady;" then she added aside: "I wouldn't own a dog," and went on her errand. Elmer was patting her foot impatiently, and muttered under her breath: "That I should be annoyed thus!"

"Don't you pity me my sweet Elmer? Why should he get ill? He has lived on nothing but fruit cake and delicacies for the year past."

"You had better show him to the doctor yourself immediately, and let him prescribe his food." Here Willet showed in the footman, a tall, sedate looking personage, who looked more fit for taking orders than taking care of dogs.

"Do you think so? As you are so very kind, I know you will pity my distress, and allow Doctor De-Tour to attend him here; it is so much nearer than Castle Place." Elmer bit her lip till the blood came, "Jonquil!"

"My Lady!"

"Tell my coachman to drive as fast as possible to Doctor De Tour's, Swiss Cottage; you know the place, and bring him here immediately."

"Yes, my Lady!"

"Tell him to bring his case of instruments and chloroform." Then turning to Elmer: "There might have to be some blood letting. You know, my dear, that 'Pinkette' and myself would both have to be put under its influence, for I certainly should faint to see the darling suffer."

"'What a pity you have no children."

"Oh, I have, my dear! but they never cause me the anxiety that this poor helpless darling does. And Jonquil, bring him a *paté de foie gras*; the poor pet may need to eat after his medicine. Quick, Jonquil."

"Yes my lady;" and the tall man bent his back like a hinge and withdrew, Willet courtesying coquettishly, but unavailingly, to him.

"How I envy you, Elmer; your mind so free from the terrible anxieties that I suffer. No sleepless nights, and loss of morning naps, no nightmare of poor suffering canines, nothing to think of but the latest novel and newest bonnet;" and she petted and caressed her dog and was oblivious to aught else. Elmer, who had torn a beautiful bouquet to pieces that stood on the table near her, walked to the window and muttered:

" Did she but know my terrible sufferings! but could a young loving heart ever have beaten in that withered bosom? Why does she not go? Oh! how I suffer!" and she threw herself impatiently on a sofa.

" I think he is slightly better. Oh! I am so thankful!"

"Well, I never!" said Willet, throwing up her hands in disgust. But the bell rang and she left the room."

" I hope that is Doctor Take-all-De-Tour."

" I trust it is;" and she added in thought, "and that I shall soon be rid of you and your puerile sorrows."

Jonquil, carrying a case of instruments, bowed in Doctor De-Tour. Fussy and the Frenchiest of French, with a dancing master's step, and an opera singer's shoulder shrug.

"Jonquil here, he tell me you want me immediate for le joli chien," Then seeing Elmer he bowed low. "Bon jour, madam!" She scarcely noticed him. "Bon jour ma ladi!" this to Lady Ashley, who was too occupied to return his salutation.

"Wat has de leetle dog?" and he took his paw and felt his pulse with all becoming gravity. "Von large fevar."

"Oh! doctor, give him the pleasantest medicine possible. I would rather pay two fees for a bread pill, provided it cured poor 'Pinkette,' than have him dosed with something unpleasant to take." But the doctor still held his paw, and took out his watch to count his pulse. Elmer looked on with contempt, but Lady Ashley was all anxiety.

"What can you do for him, dear doctor?"

"Ma ladi, him pulse beat var quick; von, two, tree, four hundred times in von sixty second."

"Poor darling! what shall we do for him?"

"Ma ladi, you take him home—" Elmer looked thankful—"and soak him four feet in varm vater, then give him some medicine vat I sall rite; put him in his leetle bed, make no much noise, and in de morning he vill be vell."

"Oh! doctor, I am so thankful that you may kiss my hand!" And as he did so, she dropped a purse into his hand.

"Merci, ma lady!" Then he wrote a perscription, and gave her. "Bon jour, madame! I have von thousand and von visit to make to-day. Bon jour!" and he bowed himself out. Jonquil took him his case, and returned with a covered dish.

"My lady, here is the patty foi gras. He had not studied French.

Willet was near the door, and she said:

"All this ado about a dog! Why, she couldn't make more fuss if it had been a handsome young man."

"I am sorry 'Pinkette' should have been so inconvenient, dear Elmer; good-by."

"Good morning, Lady Downington; I trust your terrible anxiety will soon be over." But Lady Ashley did not notice the sarcasm, and warmly shook her hand.

"Thank you, dear." She tenderly placed the dog in Jonquil's arms, then turning again to Elmer said with her former gaiety: "But please don't forget Butterfly, Rich as Crœsus, and desperately in love." And at last she went away followed by Jonquil carrying the dog as if it had been the tenderest and most precious thing in the world; this time he bowed stiffly to Willet's coquetting.

"Gone! What a relief! Oh! that I were like her; could amuse myself with a poor dog, and forget my grief."

"My lady, isn't her ladyship queer? Oh! I wouldn't be waiting maid to her for all the wealth of the Indies! What with tending her dog, and feeding her dog, and most likely rocking it to sleep, a poor girl's life would be worn out."

"You are with me, let that content you. Bring me my desk. What—what can I do to prevent his going?" Willet brought the desk, and she sat and thought; but her face soon brightened as if the thought she wanted had come, and she wrote rapidly.

"I wonder what's the matter now?" said Willet. "Oh, this love, but it does make a goose of one!"

"Take this to Sir Francis Hilton; lose no time!"

"Yes, my lady—but she's impatient," and she left the room.

Lady Elmer raised her hands to Heaven as if imploring a blessing, but her words were:

"Oh! desparate woman's guardian spirit, assist me now."

Chapter V.

Sir Francis Hilton was impatiently pacing his chambers, waiting for the earliest moment he would be allowed on the ship. He looked pale and care-worn, and several years older than he did on the night of the ball, and had he spoken his thoughts they would have been—

" This terrible uncertainty is wearing my life away. No answer to all my letters, save a few words that while her name rested under this dark cloud, it was better not to correspond; and that till she was declared innocent, I should be free. And what is free? To be unfettered by a promise, yet to be bound heart and soul by love? To wander for months, heartsick and weary, leaving nothing unattempted to obtain her release, yet all in vain? To be thousands of miles away— cruel seas and more cruel laws dividing us? Is this freedom? But to-day my heart feels lighter, for the good ship Britannia shall quickly bear me across the unkind miles, then at least I can see her again; there is happiness in the very thought."

Cubby knocked at the door, then announced Lady De Mille. Sir Francis kissed her hand, and called her "mother."

" My son!" and she embraced him; "for have you not been a son to me since my poor Clare went away? I was so impatient to send my child these little mementoes and my blessing, that I could not wait for you to come;" and she gave him a beautiful inlaid casket or box with a little key tied to it.

"My mother, would that I could take you with me. How her heart would bound with joy!"

" Only for her express wish that I should remain and see her brother on his return from India, nothing but death could separate us. Tell her he will soon be here, then, if we cannot obtain her release we will both come to her."

" Next to her release it would be the happiest news I could bring her."

" Tell her that I, her poor bereaved mother, bade her be of good cheer; that nightly my prayers ascend to Heaven for her welfare. Tell her for my sake to be as happy as she can, remembering her own innocence, and that nothing can shake our faith in her. Heaven grant you a safe and speedy voyage, and a happy meeting with my Clare! Good-by! my heart is so full that I must go and weep."

"Good-by my mother; I will remember all your loving messages!" And he kissed her forehead and led her gently to her carriage. A moment after he returned, Cubby again knocked, and being told to come in said:

"My lord, there is a young person below, who says she must see Sir Francis Hilton personally."

"I am in great haste; what can she want?"

"She did not say, my lord."

"Then show her up immediately, for I cannot waste a moment. I must not be detained for I have some business to attend to before I leave England!" Cubby showed up Willet, and bowing to her very ceremoniously left the room.

Willet courtesied and said:

"My lady sends you this letter, my lord, in great haste."

"What is your lady's name?"

"Lady Elmer Dudley." Sir Francis for reply thrust the letter angrily into his pocket.

"Is there any answer, my lord."

"None!" and he walked to the window.

"Well, his lordship isn't very polite! My lady wouldn't feel flattered if she knew how he treated her letter!" Then aloud to Cubby, who reappeared at the door, ignoring their former acquaintance:

"Young man, show me out."

"I will with pleasure, your ladyship!"

"I suppose you think you are very killing, Mr. Cubby?"

"Oh! no; I am not a butcher to kill a lamb—a catamount?"

"Umph!" and Willet flounced out of the room, followed by Cubby, who enjoyed her little display of temper.

"What can she want with me? I suppose I must read her letter;" and Sir Francis unwillingly read:

"MY GOOD FRIEND: I am compelled to go in haste to Australia, on business that I must attend to personally. I am so glad to have the opportunity of going in the same ship with a friend. I bring my maid and every—" he crushed the letter back into his pocket, "What takes her to Australia? Is it another plot against the Lady Clare, or does she take this opportunity of seeing and asking the forgiveness of the gentle being she has so deeply wronged? How shall I endure a long voyage with a woman who strangely repels yet terribly attracts and fascinates me to her, as a serpent would? As I cannot prevent her going, I will watch her every action. I suppose I must answer her letter." And he sat down to his desk, and spreading out the crumpled note finished reading it.

Chapter VI.

The ship Britannia had just left the dock, and all was bustle and confusion; the captain giving orders to the mate, the sailors setting sails, pulling ropes, and singing lively, inspiring tar songs, that one never hears but on a sailing vessel. Nearly all the passengers were waving handkerchiefs. Sir Francis was leaning pensively on the bulwarks thinking.

"The white cliffs of England will soon disappear. Oh! my dear country, shall I return to you a happy man, or as a heart broken son to his mother to die and be forgotten!" Lady Elmer came to his side, and said gently:

"Sad so soon, Sir Francis? How will you endure these long months of ocean life?"

"I shall become accustomed to, and perhaps enjoy it in a few days."

Then he turned and spoke to the captain, and Elmer saying "I hope so," walked a little distance, and looked toward shore through her opera glass.

Willet stopped waving her handkerchief suddenly and began to cry. Cubby watched her for a few moments. "Well, I can't watch this long," he thought. "Lovely woman in distress would melt the flintiest heart." Then going to her he said gently: "Willet!" But she cried the louder. "What's the matter Willet? What is it, dear Willet?" and he pulled the handkerchief from her eyes.

"To think that—I had- to leave England—for so many months—without having time to—to—"

"To what, dear Willet?"

"To—to—" still she cried.

"To bid your mother good-by?"

"No—to—"

"To see your sister?"

"No! to buy a new bonnet!" and she left him, crying angrily.

"Tut! tut! tut!" and he went to another part of the deck in disgust. Willet wiped her eyes with a great deal of show, and sniffling a little went up to Elmer and said:

"Do you think you will like this old ship, my Lady? I shan't!"

"It will be very pleasant after a few days, if we have no storms." Again she turned and looked through her glasses.

"Umph! I suppose it will for her, with the one she loves in the same house with her, as it were, and no rival near." And she watched Elmer as she lingered near Sir Francis, and saw him introduce her to the captain. "I shouldn't wonder if she caught him after all. I suppose I must make friends with that Cubby, or it will be dreadful lonely to have no one to talk to."

The captain ordered lunch to be brought to his cabin, then turning to Elmer, said:

" Lady Dudley, I have a very fine chart of the route we will take. My Lord, will you accompany us to my cabin, and I will explain it ?"

" Oh, I thank you!" said Elmer, pleased to be brought into such close company with Sir Francis.

What woman but thinks, give her the time and opportunity, that she can bring any man to her feet? And they are nearly right, too.

Sir Francis felt he must accept the invitation though he would much rather have remained alone, with his thoughts for company.

The Captain offered his arm to Elmer and they all went into his cabin.

The Captain's cabin is always a cosy, comfortable spot, easy chairs and sofas, pictures, books, fine wines, and lots of nice little things nid away; curiosities, fruits and nuts. It breaks the monotony of a long voyage to be friends with the captain. Oh ! the sea yarns he can tell ! Sinbad's adventures are scarcely more wonderful than stories I've heard these captains relate.

Willet began to experience she was not on shore.

"I—I begin to feel very faint. Will you be kind enough to help me to the cabin, Mr. Cubby? I fear I'm not a sailor."

"Oh! don't give up so soon."

"I can't help it;" and they walked to the steps leading to the cabin. "I'm so faint."

This was the first time either of them had been to sea, and the experience is not always quite pleasant; so it was not surprising that Cubby suddenly clapped his hands on his stomach, and exclaimed, looking pretty pale: "Oh, dear! and I'll keep you company." And they neither of them reappeared that day.

A long voyage on a sailing vessel makes a little isolated world of the travelers. Who that has ever taken one, can forget the friendships formed, the amusements, the little weekly paper, the concerts, the many incidents, each one a picture painted in indellible colors on the memory? Many a heart, too, has found its mate, in those romantic days, watching the ever-changing sea and sky; so few to disturb the fancy, that the one present seems the acme of perfection. It is so hard to choose, when all the world is open to our hand; like the dame who turns away and sighs at all the costly fabrics at her feet, not knowing what to choose; give the same dame a choice of two, and it is quickly made.

So our little world, the Britannia, moved on to Australia.

Chapter VII.

The day the ship arrived, Clare was at her work in the large lace factory attached to the prison.

No magnetic influence told her of the nearness of her lover. This second sight, as it were, this mind-reading, and will-compelling is very rare, and those who possess these qualities are by no means the pleasantest of companions.

She was dressed in a neat, gray merino, with white collar and cuffs, and her beautiful hair put back in a wavy roll. She was a picture as she stopped for a moment, the sunlight from the high window just gilding her hair, leaving her face in the shadow. Her head drooped as she thought :

"How wearily the time passes! Will the seven years never be over? Must the sweetest portion of my youth be passed thus? Weave, weave, as if I were destiny weaving the fate of mortals! My mother, too, though her letters try so hard to cheer me, yet I see the tears beneath her kindest words. And Sir Francis! Oh! I must not think of him till a prison ceases to be my home!" She turned quickly to her work, and sought in it oblivion from distressing thoughts.

The keeper entered with a gentleman.

"This is the lace factory," he said.   Clare raised her eyes.

"Clare!"

"Sir Francis!" and he went quickly toward her.

"No communication with the prisoners, my lord."

"Oh!" and Clare dropped her head, weeping and humiliated.

"Elmer, who had been detained a moment at the door, now entered. She saw Clare at once, and going toward her, exclaimed:

"My dear friend!"

"Lady Elmer!"   The tone was that of surprise, just touched with horror.

"Your ladyship must excuse me, but you must not speak to the prisoners without a permit."

"Is that the rule, sir?"

"It is, my lady."

"I am so sorry, for she is my friend; but I will see the Governor to-day."   She took Sir Francis' arm, and his face showed the annoyance he felt.   The keeper explained the uses of the different machines, but Sir Francis turned a yearning look to Clare, then they moved further away, and some machinery intervening, she was shut from his view.

"Oh! why are they here?   Not with my release, or they would have been allowed to speak to me.   She holds his arm so lovingly— are they married?   No, or he would not have greeted me as he did just now.   Oh! what can it mean?"   They came into view again, and she watched them eagerly.   Just then the Governor entered, and Sir Francis, after bowing, introduced him to Elmer.

"Ah! the Governor!   Sir Francis speaks to him.   He may yet obtain my release!   Oh! the joy would be too great!"

"Lady Elmer, one moment if you please."   Bowing she passed further on, and appeared to be deeply interested in the keeper's explanations. " My lord, that lady," and he pointed to Clare, " is a friend of mine.   Did you read the trial ?"

" I do not remember."

"Then I will give you a brief description."

He told him of the pretended robbery and trial, and used his best arguments to impress him favorably.   The Governor appeared struck with a sudden resolution.

" My lord, if I undertake to obtain her release, it is necessary I should have a private interview with her.   If I can do so, she shall come to England as soon as possible, accompanied by a suitable companion;" and the Governor drew him farther away from Clare.

" But surely, after coming thousands of weary miles, I must not leave her without a farewell word.

" Would not her release reward you for all your pains ?"

" Yes, a thousand times; but her gentle heart would be cruelly wounded."

"Let me explain ?" and he took him out of hearing of the others.

" Gone! without a word! has he ceased to love me?   Oh! I shall die of grief and shame!"

Elmer spoke a moment to the Governor, then rushing to Clare, threw her arms around her exclaiming:

" Oh! my poor Clare! what can I do for you ?"

But Clare stood motionless as stone, and almost as cold.

" Obtain my release," she said in a quiet, peculiar tone.

" How can I ?   I have offered half my fortune to do so, but in vain."

" Obtain my release!"

" I cannot."

" Can I be mistaken ? or is her heart stone ?" then aloud: " Lady Elmer, did you ever love ?"

"Alas! yes; so madly that I would peril my soul for a return."

" Indeed?" in a peculiar voice.

"And you love too?   Why do you not try to escape ?"

" Because I am guilty of no crime, and my trying to escape would be taken by some as proof positive of my guilt."

" But think; seven weary years to spend in this dreadful place. Your companions thieves and murderers; your mother longing to clasp you in her arms; your friends waiting for your return.

"And Sir Francis ?"   But Elmer sighed and drooped her head. " What means that sigh?   Does he believe me guilty ?   If he does, the prison has no more terror for me."

" Oh! do not ask me, but try to escape."

" If Sir Francis thinks me guilty, I have no desire to live—but I would see my poor mother, and die upon her breast."   And Clare wept so despairingly that it touched even Elmer.

" Does my heart relent ?   I must leave her or be lost!" and she hurried from her side.

Sir Francis and the Governor approached Clare.

" You will allow me to speak to her now, and I will leave Australia on the ship that departs to-morrow."

"Certainly; I will remain here;" and he turned to Lady Elmer, who soon appeared to be deeply interested in his description of this wonderful, beautiful country, in which she would remain but such a short time.   Yet not a movement of Sir Francis or Clare escaped her subtle glance.

Sir Francis had warmly greeted Clare.

" Oh! my Clare, once more I clasp your hand, and—" he looked defiantly at Elmer—" I care not."   And he folded her in his arms.

" Oh, my heart's chosen, how I have suffered !"

"And I, too!" weeping, her head drooped on his shoulder.

"Oh! do not weep.   When I have traveled thousands of miles for this happy moment, do not let me see tears in the eyes I so love ; for dearest, not for one moment has a doubt of your innocence crossed my mind."

"Then I am happy, even though a prison's walls surround me. And my mother! you saw her; is she well? What message did she send?"

"Her undying love. She bids you be of good cheer. That when your brother returns, if they cannot obtain your release, they will both come to you."   .

"You bring me joyful news, indeed. Oh! I can bear up now, and pity from my heart, the poor beings around me who have not my hopes to sustain them."

"I have spoken to the Governor so that you will not be compelled to work."

"Oh! Sir Francis, that was not a kindness! I should think myself to death were I forced to be idle. Let me weave my lace, it has been my friend, my comforter, when my heart was almost breaking."

"You shall keep your friend. I can easily imagine it has saved you many an hour of heartache, for enforced idleness adds bitterly to mental pain. Your dear mother sends you a casket containing some remembrances. I will have it brought to you when you return to your room, for you will leave your lace for the rest of the day, surely."

"Oh! yes; I have no need of such a friend now. When you return, take my mother my dearest love. Tell her that I will try to bear up for her sweet sake!"

The factory bell rang loudly, and the girls and women began to move out in a slow, melancholy line.

"That is the dinner bell, and it is my greatest trial to eat before all these staring eyes, some that exult to see me here, few that look in pity." The Governor and Elmer now joined them.

"My lord, please let me dine alone to-day?" and Clare looked beseechingly into his face.

"Certainly, your ladyship, and every day if you choose."

"Oh, thanks!"

"Farewell, Clare, till we meet again!" and Sir Francis left her with a kiss on her hand; but Elmer turned away without a word, the spirit of a demon in her heart.

Chapter VIII.

Clare's cell was a small room, furnished with a neat bed and several chairs, a strip of matting, a few prints without frames, and a vase of flowers. White curtains, held back with blue ribbons, graced the window, and a few ornaments and books on a table, took away the prison look and made it quite homelike, thanks to her friend, the sweet Beatrice, the Governor's fair and only daughter.

Clare had hastened here, awaiting the coming of the casket, and now sat with her head resting on her hand.

"Am I really awake ? or is this but a dream—a dream of happiness to cheat me awhile from sorrow ?"

Beatrice knocked gently at the door, then came in.

"See, dear Clare, what I have for you;" and she held up the beautiful box. " The gentleman brought it all the way from England. I heard him tell papa about it ; then I kissed papa and asked him to let me bring it to you. Now give me my pay and I'll be off and leave you— just fifteen minutes to look at the pretty things it contains, then I'm coming back to see them, too."

Clare kissed her and said :

" You are as angelic as your namesake. Come, and share my happiness."

" I will," and she disappeared like a sunbeam. " Every cloud has a silver lining ; that dear girl is my cloud's silver lining." She held up the casket. " How familiar it looks ; in an instant it carries me back to home and friends again. I know it's spring so well." And she pressed a little golden rose and the lid flew up. She took from it a long gold chain, to which was attached an old fashioned medallion, surrounded with pearls and diamonds.

" My mother's portrait; dear, dear face, and kind, loving eyes. Are they dimmed now by the many tears shed for your poor Clare ? They shall brighten quickly, for Hope whispers I shall soon be free. Here is my own little watch ; how thoughtful. What is this ? My Bible ! I had forgotten it and the comfort it would bring me." She opened the golden clasp, and there, inside, lay a letter and a lock of her mother's hair. She kissed them both, then read the letter.

" MY DEAR CHILD : Nothing shall shake our faith in you. When you return, we will leave cold, cruel England, and live in beautiful Venice, away from all our trials. You shall not have another unhappy moment if a mother's loving heart can keep you from it. Do not despond. I am only waiting your brother's return, then we will fly to you, to bear you from that dreadful place or remain with you. Heaven bless you always. Your loving, hoping Mother."

And Clare wept tears that relieved her over-burdened heart.

Beatrice knocked gently at the door, then entered.

" Fifteen minutes up. Weeping ! I hope that pretty box did not cause those tears."

"They were only caused by joy dear friend. There, they shall not annoy you."

" See what I have brought you ; roses for your hair ;" and she took out Clare's comb, and her beautiful hair fell in a shower below her waist ; then she fastened it back with the roses and pinned a bouquet in her dress. " Now let me see the pretties in this box, and find something more to adorn my queen. Yes, this beautiful chain ; it is your mother's portrait ; I can tell, because it has eyes just like yours." And she kissed it and talked to it as if it were alive. "Dear mother of my dear friend, I love you already. Now the watch ; and see, here in the corner is a beautiful diamond ring. Hold out your dainty, lily-white hand. Now, who looks like a princess ?"

"You are a dear girl, and your friendship has kept me from despair! But tell me why you have arrayed me thus ?"

"Oh! it's not to see the handsome gentleman who brought the box, but to go with me to my father; he wishes to see you on important business, and I'm to be your guard. I'm to be held responsible for you—isn't that funny? They wouldn't trust me, if they knew I would cry with joy for a week, if you would only run away! Will you see my father ?"

"Oh! yes! perhaps he has my release."

"I'll run and bring our carriage, then." And she was gone.

"So much joy in one day. Does happiness ever whiten one's hair! I can soon see, for here in the cover of the box is my little looking glass; I had forgotten it. I almost fear to look. I wonder if I am much altered? Six months! have the roses left my cheeks?" She bent her head to look but stopped. "Suppose I see wrinkles; that always makes a woman sad—I won't look; I haven't the courage." And she shut the box. But her woman's curiosity was strong. "And yet—and yet—" she unconsciously touched the spring and the lid flew up, as Beatrice entered.

"The carriage is here, dear; throw this around you," and she gave Clare a large black lace mantle, which she threw around her, partly covering her head, as the Spanish ladies do. "How pretty you look! here," and she caught the box from the table, and held the glass before her; "see for yourself."

"My hair is not white yet! Oh! I'm so glad!"

"What! have you been dreaming away fifty years, to think of such a thing? No, indeed; your hair is as brown, and your cheeks as rosy, as when you first came here."

"Then let us go quickly, for I so long to be free!"

She left the prison with such bright hopes, pulses high, cheeks flushed. Were they to be realized? A disappointment now would almost kill her.

Chapter IX.

Outside the jail, on the sea shore, Cubby and Willett were taking a walk. Willet had determined to secure a husband before she returned to England ; she was also determined that husband should be Cubby. Now, when a woman makes up her mind upon such a subject, a man may as well surrender at once, for his fate is as inevitable as if proclaimed by the ruling stars. They were talking of things far removed from love—porpoises—but she would lead him to it soon, trust her woman's tact.

"Yes, my dear Willet," he said, "they are the strangest people here you ever heard tell of. Only think ! They wouldn't kill one of those great, fat, ugly purpoises for anything."

"La! why not ?"

"Because they think the spirits of their dead friends go into them."

"How heathenish !"

"Yes ; in the boat this morning, I was about to play a trick on one and catch him in the nose with a little hook, when Jack Jordan nearly pushed me out of the boat."

"The brute ! What for ?"

"Don't ye dare hurt him," he said ; "that's Bill Jones' brother." So none of them would speak to me for the rest of the sail, except so cross and surly and short, that I was glad when we landed."

" Don't expose your precious life with those barbarians any more. It's very romantic here, though, isn't it Cubby ?   The great big waves rolling up to your feet, and the lobster shells lying around !"

" Yes, and the smell of the sea breeze, as if one had a barrel of herring in their cellar.   But my lord leaves on the ship to-morrow, which doesn't please me.   Six months on sea to one on land isn't just the ticket."

" La ! you don't say so !   And does my lady leave, too ?"

" You ought to know that !   Why, you couldn't keep her from going in the ship he sails in, for—for—I don't know what simile to make. I thought you were clever enough to see that."

But she smiled and said :

" Well, you know, sometimes it's politics to be blind."

" Yes, and dumb, too ; well, then, we leave on the ship to-morrow, and the friend doesn't go with us, as far as I can understand."

" You mean Lady Clare, the poor dear ! I'd like to see her so much, and say a kind word to her.   How can I arrange it ?"

" I'm sure I don't know.   Why not ask your lady ?   If she says no, get a rope ladder and we will scale the building."

" Why, Cubby, dear, when did you get to be so romantic ?"

" Three months of your charming society on the briny deep would make a very fish romantic."

" I do believe the poor fellow's getting in love !   La, Cubby do you find my society charming ?"

" I do here; I don't know how it will be when we get back to England."

" Well I never ! I must attach him a little stronger to me.   Cubby, who was that handsome fellow painting carriages in the room they left us in yesterday ?"

" Hey ?   Some thief, or perhaps murderer in the second degree."

" That can't be !   I believe he's under a false charge.   Why, he has birds and flowers in the room, and was humming. What a sweet smile he has."

" Hey? What's he to you?"

"Oh! nothing, of course! but one may admire anything handsome, mayn't they, in nature or art?"

"Perhaps you could persuade him to try for a 'ticket-of-leave' and come over to England."

"Well, what would be the harm if I did? I am sure it would be a very charitable thing to do."

"Miss Sarah Willet!" and he took her hand from his arm, "would you as leave take the rest of your walk alone?"

Putting her hand back on his arm, she replied: "I would just as leave walk with you."

"Then just please to remember not to mention birds, flowers, or sweet smiles to me again."

"I do believe Cubby's getting jealous."

"No such thing! no such thing! but if you want to admire anybody, admire me. You" but she laughed so heartily, that he said no more, but hurried her on with their walk in silence.

Thus destiny was weaving a little romance for our humbler sister, without all the pain, anguish, and crime, the elegant lady, her mistress, was enduring and committing to bring one man to her feet.

Why is it that some people are happy without an effort of their own, the good things of this world poured into their lap, sorrow and pain passing harmless by their houses, as they did those of old, marked with the blood, while others, with heart and brain so sensitive and capable of happiness, with minds highly cultured, pulses passionate, beings capable of intense love, and worthy of it—why should they so often suffer the tortures of the damned? Yet so it is. Poor imbecility is happy, while beings that should reign are, like the archangel of old, cast down into the lower depths, their hearts gnawing their very lives away, and their ambition trailing like mantles in the dirt.

Chapter X.

The Governor sat in his elegant parlor, thinking.

"Young, fair looking, wealthy, a fine old name and innocent. Not a bad investment; then, too, an act of charity, and I'm not so old that her loving me some day should be an impossibility." With this he walked to the mantle-glass to see how he really did look. "Hair slightly gray, umph—well, a very few wrinkles; not so bad! not so bad! I think if she were my wife, I could persuade her gracious Majesty of her entire innocence.

"Then, too, I should not be worried with the complaints of a grown up daughter when the step-mother happens to be young and fair, for Beatrice loves her more than I do at present."

He turned with a smile from the glass, as Beatrice ran in and threw her arms about his neck. Clare stood in the doorway.

"Dear papa, here's my Clare, looking oh! so sweet. I hope you will love her as I do, and let her go home on a beautiful ship. But I shall cry when she goes, indeed I shall!" and she ran to the door and brought Clare to where her father stood.

The Governor bowed low.

"I am sorry, Lady Clare, that you did not make yourself known to me before. I should have tried to have made your unjust imprisonment a little more comfortable. You see with so many we cannot individualize, unless there is some peculiarity in their case which is brought to our notice. From what your friend Sir Francis Hilton says, I believe you are entirely innocent of the charge for which you are imprisoned."

"Oh! my lord, I thank you!" and she kissed his hand. "Thank you!" and she could not prevent the tears coming.

"Don't cry, for I'm so happy," said Beatrice, kissing her.

"I believe every effort was made in England to obtain your release?" Clare bowed. "And all were unsuccessful?"

"Yes."

"I have been thinking what influence I could bring to bear for your speedy release, greater than your family or Sir Francis Hilton exerted, and I have decided that there is at least one fair chance untried."

"Oh! what is it, my lord? You will have my mother's fervent prayers, and Sir Francis Hilton's eternal gratitude."

"And you?"

"My life's devotion!" He looked pleased, but when she added "I will love you as my dear father," he was a little annoyed.

"Beatrice!" he called, and beckoned for her to bring some refreshments.

"Yes, papa; here is some cake, and some cordial that I made myself. Take some, dear Clare, I want to drink your health."

"My dear Beatrice, I could not now."

"Do my dear young lady, it will strengthen you to hear my plan, and decide what you think best." So they each took a small glass of the fragrant cordial, and he said: "Here's to your speedy release!"

"I hope so!" cried Beatrice as joyfully as if the release was sure to come now that her father interested himself in her friend. Clare smiled her thanks to both. The Governor placed her in an elegant easy chair, and sat down beside her while Beatrice went to the window, and appeared to be much interested in what was going on outside.

"It may appear abrupt, this sudden declaration of interest on my part," said the Governor, "but if it obtains for you your desired release, you will not think it the less worthy of attention. Beatrice there—oh! I know you're listening, you little rogue—loves you dearly already, so you would not come a stranger into this house."

"I—I do not understand."

"I—I—mean—" Beatrice relieved him of his embarrassment by throwing her arms around Clare, and exclaiming:

"Papa means for you to marry him! Oh! do, dear Clare."

"Surely you cannot mean that?" said Clare, rising in agitation.

"Why not? Am I so repulsive that I never need hope to marry again?"

"Oh! no, my lord, but I am the betrothed wife of Sir Francis Hilton!"

"And what of that? Has he been able to obtain your release?"

"Alas, no!"

"Then marry me and see what a devoted husband can do. I will so besiege and entreat her Majesty, that she will be compelled to believe in your innocence."

"But I love Sir Francis."

"Time will cure that. He leaves Australia to-morrow."

"To-morrow! without a farewell word? Oh! I did not believe he could be so cruel! My lord, I will go back to my prison; liberty is not so precious now."

Beatrice came to her and said in a pleading manner:

"Don't say no, dear Clare; if you marry papa you will never leave us, and that would make me so happy."

"Beatrice, you do not know what love is, or you would not urge me to marry your father without it, and my heart filled with devotion for another."

"I will not urge my suit now, Lady Clare, but trust to time and your own good sense to help me; for should the Queen refuse to hear me, you would only be a prisoner in name, for as my wife you would have the freedom of the whole island, none here daring to question me."

The bell rang violently.   Beatrice ran to the window and cried:

"Oh! papa, there is a lady at the door in deep black, with a heavy vail over her face.   What can she want?"

A servant entered and said a lady wished to see the Governor.

"Tell her I am engaged."

"No, my lord, let me return to my prison; I feel very weary."

"Show her up!" said the Governor not very well pleased.

"I'll go to the carriage with you, dear, Clare, then I'm coming back to see what she wants."   By this time Lady Elmer stood in the door; seeing Clare she startled and muttered:

"Am I too late?" But she bowed low as Clare and Beatrice passed her.

Clare thought, "what brings her here? Can it be treachery?" but said not a word as she returned the bow and left the room.

"Your business with me, madam? said the Governor as he handed her a chair.

"You have a prisoner there," and she pointed to the prison.   She spoke quietly, but could not hide agitation.   "A titled lady."

"That is true, madam."

"Her name is Clare De Mille."

"Again correct, madam."

"The lady's lover has just traveled several thousand miles; most likely to effect her escape."

"Ah! there your knowledge exceeds mine."

"I come to request you to redouble your vigilance till the ship leaves to-morrow."

"Indeed! that is a singular request from a stranger.   How can the lady's escape or detention affect you?"

She started to her feet.

"More than life itself! Oh! I—I—cannot explain. You are a widower, are you not?"

"I have that unhappiness, madam." Here Beatrice came quietly into the room, and sat down apart from them.

"Then marry this girl, and I will give her a dowry of twenty thousand pounds."

"I have already done myself the honor of proposing."

"Did she refuse?"

"She loves another."

"Then marry her to any one—a common thief, if need be, and I will give you thirty thousand pounds."

"How do I know but that you are the lady in disguise?" and he snatched the heavy vail quickly from her face. "Ah! Lady Elmer Dudley! I am happy to see you, madam!" and he bowed low.

"How dare you?" But she saw that she was discovered, and that anger would be bad policy, so she said humbly: "Now you know who I am you can understand my motives."

"You a—you love Sir Francis Hilton?"

"Alas! yes!" Beatrice shocked, hurried from the room to seek and inform Clare.

"I will tell you for your own satisfaction, Lady Dudley, if by any means I can induce the Lady Clare to become my wife, I shall do so."

"If she does not consent *compel* her to. Tell her Sir Francis is to be married on his return to England; anything to make her hate him."

Here a servant brought word that Sir Francis Hilton wished to speak to the Governor.

"Oh! he must not see me here; it would ruin my prospects forever. Where can I go?"

"Step into my daughter's room for a moment."

She quickly covered her face with the heavy vail, and went into the room; but standing near the door, she listened intently, and heard nearly all that passed between Sir Francis and the Governor.

How her heart bounded with hope, as she heard the Governor request Sir Francis not to see the Lady Clare again before his departure
as it might interfere with his plans for her release.   Sir Francis
suffered torture at the thought, but at last consented.

"For her sake, I would suffer as the martyrs did of old."   But
during the long interview no kind word for Elmer escaped his lips,
and she bit her hand till it bled, as he left the house without once
mentioning her name.

Chapter XI.

It was nearly sunset and the yellow light gilded the prison till it
seemed almost a thing of beauty; the waves tipped with golden fire,
washed its base, and the clouds spread in glory above it.   Yet behind
those shining walls, grief, misery, and crime, everything that was bad in
human nature, and but little that was pure and good, had their abode.

Sir Francis was on the beach, intently watching the scene.

"There is the grim monster that hides my Clare, and should the
Governor's artempt fail, when shall I see her again ?   Oh, it almost
tempts me to make confidants of thieves and vagabonds to learn their
profession, so   that   I   might   scale those walls and bear my   darling
hence, away from the tyranny of cruel laws to some fair southern isle,
never to see England or Lady Dudley again.   What brought her here ?
That thought troubles me, for she has attended to no business as yet,
and says she leaves on the ship to-morrow.   Is she in league with
some one to destroy the Lady Clare ?   How powerless I am to ascertain or prevent it !   Creatures of destiny, all of us !   Wealth and
titles, often, as futile to obtain a desired object as the gauntest poverty.
I must leave this spot or I shall be tempted to break my word with the
Governor, and see her once more, despite the consequences !"   As

he was thinking thus, Willet, who was seeking him, came near and coughed, to attract his attention, and when he looked at her she courtesied and said :

" My lord, my lady wishes to know if your time is all engaged this afternoon ?"

" Must that woman haunt me like the recollection of some terrible nightmare ?" Then turning to her he said aloud: " Yes, till the ship sails."

" How ungracious ! She hasn't done much toward catching him, after all ; but I must be polite, as I expect to enter his lordship's service as Mrs. Cubby, on our return to dear England ;" then she courtesied and said : " Thank you, your lordship. I will tell her your time is all engaged ;" and she started to walk away.

" What can she want to see me for? Should it be about poor Clare! Oh ! I must not neglect the least trifle that points to her release. Stay !" he called to Willet ; " tell her I will see her in an hour," and he walked rapidly away.

" Well, he's a fickle gentleman, whatever they may say about the ladies. I hope the air of England won't cause me and Mr. Cubby to alter our determination ;" and she hurried back to her lady, bringing joy to her torn, passionate heart, for like a discreet servant, she only told what was pleasant, keeping the rest to herself.

Chapter XII.

Beatrice had hurried to ascertain what she could, then gone to Clare, and was standing and talking excitedly, while she listened, looking, oh ! so sad and despondent.

" Yes, you must escape this very day, for oh ! you don't know what that bad woman said ; ' marry her to a common thief, if need be, and I will give you thirty thousand pounds!'   Oh, my Clare, there is a price set upon your head ; you are to be sold like a slave in the market-place !   But I will prevent it !   I have secured my brother's boat in a little secret grotto that I discovered, almost at the prison door, and have formed plans for your escape.   You take this knotted rope ; your love of life and liberty will teach you what to do."

"Oh, Beatrice, I am innocent ; if I try to escape they will deem me guilty."

Oh, do not, do not remain for that unscrupulous woman to plot against you."

" What have I done to any human being that they should destroy me thus ?"

" Dear Clare, no matter how innocent you are, it seems you cannot obtain your release legally, so unless you escape, you must remain here the rest of those long, weary years ; subjected, too, to annoy-ances that will break your gentle heart.   For the love I bear you, do not refuse this chance of liberty.   I will put food and clothing in the boat, and will join you before the moon rises.   Oh, I almost forgot this letter."

" Ah! it is Sir Francis' writing."   She took it and read the contents eagerly, her eyes quickly filling with tears.   " Beatrice, I shall not see him again till we meet in England, and how can I endure to go there, having to lurk in lanes and alleys, not daring to go to my home, or even to the church, for fear of recognition.   A fearful dread haunting me, of a heavy hand upon my shoulder, and the deadening words, ' you are my prisoner!' hissed in my ears, blasting life and hope ! Oh! what would liberty be at such a price ?"

" Dear Clare, you look upon the darkest side.   Go to beautiful, free America; there marry Sir Francis, and remain till your innocence is declared as it must be, will be, before long.   Do not remain here to let that bad woman undermine your happiness, and perhaps even marry your betrothed."

"Sir Francis loves me too dearly for that ever to happen. See what his letter says: ' My beloved, not even death shall part us, for should you go before, a broken heart would soon hurry me after. Let nothing shake your faith in me!' And nothing shall."

" But, dear friend, he will soon be gone, and she may leave a bribe with one of the prisoners to do you personal harm. Think how desperate a woman could act, loving wildly, but with that love unreturned. Nothing would be impossible to her. And see! even now she meets him on the beach, and detains him against his will. He looks here as if beseeching you to come." They were both at the barred window, and could see Elmer talking to Sir Francis with drooping head.

Clare's heart gave a great bound, and the spirit of resistance came to aid her; she cried:

"I will crush that woman's evil plans, come what may. To-night I escape."

The sun had set and clouds covered the sky. Beatrice had placed some provisions and shawls in the boat, but nothing for a long voyage, or as a protection from danger. She was only a young girl with a heart filled with love for her friend, and an enthusiastic desire for her escape.

When all was quiet at the prison, and the lights out, Beatrice stood beneath Clare's window. She clapped her hands three times, but not very loud, then called in a whisper:

" Clare, Clare!" She appeared directly at the small window, where they had bent two of the bars, so that she could press her slender body through the space.

" Is everything ready ?" she asked in a loud whisper.

"Yes. Quick, the guard is at the furthest wall."

Clare threw out the rope. "Hold it firmly, I have secured this end so that I can easily descend." She had passed it twice around the post of the bedstead, which she had drawn close to the window ; then she had made a loop at the end for her foot, and another further above for her hand.

As she appeared out of the window, Beatrice's heart beat fast; suppose her strength should fail, and she should let go of the rope, her dear friend would be dashed to pieces. The thought was horrible and made her blood rush through her veins. As Clare began to descend, she had to exert all her strength and play the rope out very slowly. As the wind caught her white garments she looked like an angel floating in the air. When she had descended half the distance the moon broke from a cloud, and bathed her in silvery light.

"We shall be discovered," almost shrieked Beatrice.

"Quicker, then, I am not afraid!" Fear of discovery gave Beatrice almost superhuman strength, and in a few moments more Clare touched the earth. The friends clasped each other in a warm embrace, then thanking God for her escape, they hurried into the boat, and in a few moments they were on the broad ocean, breathing the air of liberty.

Chapter XIII.

The morrow had come, and the ship had started on her voyage to England. And now it was night, and the moon lit up the scene, making it supremely beautiful. But Sir Francis' eyes were turned inward, reading his heart's book; he saw nothing of his surroundings. Elmer was walking with the Captain, and Cubby and Willet were playing their little romance. The sailors were pulling some ropes and singing the musical tar song the words of which were incomprehensible to all save the singer.

> "Blow the man down, bullies, hey, hey!
> Blow the man down.
> Roll him, groll him, hearties, ho,
> Give me some time to blow the man down."

Sir Francis thought :

"Each moment bears me farther from her, powerless to snatch her from that wretched prison, or share it with her !" and he leaned over the bulwarks and looked yearningly at the land they had left.

"Is it not a lovely night, Captain ?" said Elmer sweetly, and with a subtle woman's policy, trying to show Sir Francis that she could take pleasure in another's society.

"Yes; but do you see yonder small black cloud ?"

"Where ?"

"There."

"But surely that is not large enough to cause us any inconvenience."

"Ah! my lady, in a short time you will hear these old sails and ropes speak in tones not to be mistaken."

"Do you really think there will be any danger, Captain?" But here the faint thunder rolled a long peal through the sky.

"It may blow over, the moon still shines."

"I hope so; a storm at sea must be very unpleasant," she said nervously.

" Excuse me; I must watch that cloud closely;" and he took his glass and looked, and then moved away.

Elmer went timidly to Sir Francis' side. "Sir Francis, do you think there will be much of a storm ?"

"Why the moon is shining."

"Yes, but see that black cloud; how rapidly it is approaching us." The thunder rolled louder. "It makes me nervous."

"I wish the lightning would flash and the thunder roar, and the waves dash mountains high! something in unison with my feelings."

"How can you wish it!" and she shuddered as the thunder came louder, and walked away.

"Oh, I hope there isn't going to be a storm!" said Willet.

"Don't be a goose, you little duck! it's nice to watch the lightning flash, and hear the thunder roar if there isn't too much of it!" replied Alphonse Cubby.

"Any of it's too much for me! I don't think I shall ever venture on the sea again."

"What would you do if I should become the captain of a goodly ship?"

"Willet!" called Elmer, from the bulwark where she had been looking off with her glass.

"My lady!"

"Look through these glasses and tell me is it not a boat you see."

"Where?"

"There, there; do you not see it?"

"Yes—oh, yes! I see it now; and—and there is some one in it."

"Man or woman?"

"It is too large for one person, it's—it's two women."

"I thought so!" and she took the glasses and looked through them eagerly. "It is Clare; she has made her escape!" But the thunder rolled so heavily that she started and dropped the glasses, then shuddering she hid her head in her shawl.

Sir Francis who had also been looking through his glass, called:

"Captain, one moment if you please. Are there not two women in that boat?" The Captain brought his powerful glass to bear upon the boat, and after looking a few moments said:

"Yes, and they are in distress; do you not see that signal fluttering wildly in the wind? Take my glass, most likely it is more powerful." He took it, and in a moment exclaimed: "It is Clare, and some one with her! Oh, they will be lost in this storm! Captain, what can we do ?" But the little cloud had increased in size till it nearly covered the sky and shut out the light of the moon; the thunder was very heavy and the lightning kept up a continual flash, and the rain began to fall in torrents

"It is so dark that I would have to trust to the flashes of lightning to find them." A terrible peal of thunder decided him. "I will make the attempt. Man the life boat!"

"Captain, I'm one of the crew!" cried Sir Francis. Elmer heard it amid all the confusion of sailors running hither and thither, Truman, the mate, shouting orders, the pulling of ropes, and the din of the tempest. She would not have left the deck now, if almost instant death were the penalty. Her love was stronger than her fear.

"Captain!" she called in a loud whisper, "twenty thousand pounds to leave them to their fate!"

"But they will be lost."

"So much the better; a—some other ship may save them. Thirty thousand pounds if you do not hesitate."

"I'm poor and mortal—stay, my men, we will not risk it."

"Ah!" Elmer exclaimed in joyous triumph.

But Sir Francis had been watching her, and suspected she had caused the captain to countermand the order.

'Treachery!" he cried, throwing off his coat, and leaping overboard, as the thunder with a fearful crash seemed to rend the very heavens, and the lightning to change the dark ocean into an abyss of fire.

Elmer shrieked and rushed wildly to the side of the vessel, but before she reached the bulwarks, she fainted and fell to the deck.

"Oh, my poor lady, she is dead!" cried Willet, in a moment at her side.

"Quick, bring her to my cabin, and get the doctor." They did so, and one of the sailors called the doctor. But Truman, suspecting something was wrong, said:

"My men, lower the boat; that man and those women must be be saved."

And the sailors who were kind hearted, were glad and cried:

"Ay, ay, sir!" and singing, they lowered the boat, as the cloud passed on, and the moon was shining.

Chapter XVI.

There, in the little boat, with the waves surging around them, was Clare, holding Beatrice in her arms. A handkerchief was tied to an oar as a signal of distress, and so they waited; and now the moon shone on them

"Does the ship see us?" asked Beatrice in a faint voice.

"Not yet, I think."

"Oh, I'm so cold! The storm has wet me to the skin!"

"I, too, am drenched, so cannot help you. Are you still thirsty?"

"I do not suffer so, as the rain you so thoughtfully caught in your hands, so much refreshed me."

"Poor child! I gave it to her while my throat was parched!" A distant peal of thunder caused Beatrice to tremble.

"Oh! is not the storm over? The lightning frightens me so."

"Yes, dear Beatrice, it has passed and the moon shines; that is only its dying moan. Oh, the storm was grand. I am sorry you were so terrified; you lost a glorious sight."

"How brave you are. Dear Clare, had it not been for you I should have died with terror. What is that? I hear distant singing."

"It is from the ship—it is nearing us!" and she shaded her eyes with her hand and looked intently.

"But do they see us?"

" I cannot tell yet."

" Had I not lost the other oar in my terror, we might at least have made an effort for our lives. Oh, I am so faint."

" How shall I attract their attention ? Could they hear if I should sing ? But my throat is parched, so long without water; forgetting to put any in the boat." Beatrice sighed, and her head sank on Clare's shoulder. " I'll try;" and she sang a sweet plaintive air—a mother's love; and pausing every little while she listened. As her sweet voice died away she heard a sound.

" Ah !" she exclaimed joyfully, " I hear the dipping of oars; they come—nearer and nearer—we are saved !" At a distance Truman cried:

" Cheer up, my lassies !"

" Do you hear, Beatrice ? The boat is nearly here, to bear us to the ship and safety."

" What is it ? Oh, I was dreaming so pleasantly. A boat did you say ?"

" Yes, it is nearly here! But should they recognize me, would they send me back again ? Kind Heaven forbid it and protect me !" And now the boat with Truman and the sailors in it, was near to theirs. Truman cried in a cheering voice:

" You are all right, my lassies, and will soon be safe in the warm ship—what's that, a sick one ?"

" Yes; we are nearly exhausted; bear her tenderly."

" Ay, ay! my lass! But I'm sorry to tell ye, ye'll both have to be stowaways."

" For what reason ?"

" There's a lady on board who's no friend of yours, for after whispering to the Captain, he countermanded the order to ' man the life boat!' "

" It is Lady Elmer. Will she hunt me to the death ?"

But Truman quickly helped them into the boat and ordered his men to pull away for their lives.

As they were quickly nearing the ship, Sir Francis swam in sight of Clare's boat. He was nearly exhausted, buffeting the waves.

" Where is she ? I—I cannot go much farther. Ah! here is the boat—empty! Clare lost!" His hands loosened themselves from the boat and he sank. In a moment more the second boat from the ship reached him. The officer commanding it cried: " Hearties, he went down this moment—here." And as he spoke, Sir Francis rose and grasped the empty boat. The sailors quickly pulled him into theirs, but he lay lifeless.

" Is he dead ?" asked the officer.

"Dead !" the men replied, and sadly and in silence they rowed to the ship.

Chapter XV.

Poor Clare and the gentle Beatrice were stowed away in hiding places for three long months, only coming on deck at night, when the passengers were all asleep, and the captain had retired. Clare knew nothing of Sir Francis' effort to save her, and how he nearly lost his life, and how the doctor had, with the greatest difficulty, resuscitated him.

The ship was near her journey's end, and all was joyous bustle and excitement. The poor girls could hear it, and it made them feel so sad and lonely that they could not stand upon the deck and watch the nearing shore. But Truman and the sailors did all in their power to make them comfortable and to feel less lonely. They would bring them sailor's knots made of different colored ribbons, little articles whittled out of wood, rings made of coal and bone. The last presents they brought were two little ships, perfect in construction, and named after them. Truman had bought them a couple of warm shawls from some of the passengers, and each day had supplied them with good food, and nuts, and dried fruit, and took them on the deck at night. They were very grateful, and his name was wafted up to heaven with their every prayer.

The ship landed at the dock, and after all the passengers were ashore and the men were busy bringing out the freight, Truman, with Clare and Beatrice, left the ship.

Clare had written, by Truman's advice, a letter to her mother, telling her of her escape, and to come for her, at a certain obscure inn, in a close carriage and at night, so as not to risk a re-arrest.

The inn, the Golden Hen, was in a small street not far from the Dudley mansion. She had asked Truman to find one as near there as possible. Beatrice was to return in a ship that sailed for Australia in an hour, so now they had to part.

"Truman, you have been a kind, true friend ; take my little watch, and let its ticking always remind you how grateful I feel for the good you have done to a poor, unhappy girl, who, but for you, would now be at the bottom of the sea." She grasped his hand and covered it with tears and kisses ; and he, poor fellow, turned away his head and wiped his eyes upon his sleeve.

Then the two girls clasped each other in a close embrace.

"Oh ! dear Clare, it makes me so unhappy to leave you. I thought at least to see you safe with your mother. But my father must be suffering, for I am his only daughter and he loves me dearly ; but I left a letter for him, saying how my deep affection for you compelled me to aid in your escape, and that I would return on the first vessel that sailed after seeing you safe in England."

"Good-by, Beatrice, and believe your love is not wasted, for you occupy the place next my mother and Sir Francis." She pressed on her finger her beautiful diamond ring. "Those stones are not more enduring than my love for you, and their brightness will sooner fade than my gratitude." Once more they embraced, promising to write soon and often. Then Truman put Clare into a cab, and, in a moment, amid tears and kisses, the friends who had been for three long months all the world to each other, were parted.

Chapter XVI.

It was night, and Sir Francis and Elmer were on their way to Lady De Mille's. She had begged to be allowed to accompany him, and he had been forced, though unwillingly, to consent.

''We will tell Lady De Mille we saw the Lady Clare in health and as beautiful as ever," said Sir Francis.

" And how sorry we are that we bring no hopes of a speedy release."

" The poor girls in the boat, who could they have been?" and he looked intently in Elmer's face. She starting slightly, said:

"Why how should I know?"

"The captain was a villain to countermand his orders."

"Yes, after I had spoken to him, too."

"Could I have been mistaken?" he thought. "You had spoken to him?"

"Yes, did you not see us?" He had been so intent on watching her, that he had unconsciously slacked his pace, and they were now walking slowly. It was a rather common part of the town, the street they were now on, filled with cheap shops and pawnbroker's places, those friends, though hard ones, of the poor.

Clare found on her arrival at the inn, that she had only sufficient money to pay the cab hire, and when night came, and still she heard nothing from her mother, she decided to search for a pawnbroker's—a place she had read about in novels, and had seen from her carriage window—but to enter one! Her heart sank at the thought; but necessity compelled her, so with the shawl that Truman gave her, over her head, she crept along the streets, like any other poor wretch. Thus it was, on nearing the shop she was looking for, she saw her lover and Lady Elmer. She started in horror.

"Oh! they are together! She is trying to rob me of his love!"

"See how that woman is watching us. Can her object be robbery?" whispered Elmer tightening her hold on Sir Francis' arm. Clare stepped back.

"No; 'tis some poor woman seeking the pawnshop, most likely, whom we have frightened away."

"Do you think so? I am quite nervous since that dreadful storm."

"Poor creature !" said Sir Francis, looking at Clare ; they then walked quickly away.

"He pities me as though I were some creature of the streets !" and her tears came thick and fast. "Had it not been better to have died that night in the glory of the storm? I dare not reveal myself to him, for Elmer would discover it and denounce me. Nothing left for my present support but the little money I may get for my mother's portrait!" and she took it from her bosom and kissed and talked to it. "Mother you will forgive me, when you know it is to save my life. I am almost afraid to go into this shop;" and she looked into the window. "The man is so fierce looking; will he try to harm me?"

As she stood by the door, undecided whether to enter or not, a young ruffian, half thief and loafer, accosted her. "Hi! Runabout, what you got there? Give it me!" and he snatched at the long chain, but she held it tightly, and uttering a slight scream she cried:

"I need it to get bread !"

"Then come in and let me introduce you to my Uncle; he'll give you mor'n a bob and a tanner for that trinket!" and he caught hold of her arm.

"Oh! let me go, do, you frighten me."

"Come, come, none of your slack, or I'll take that trinket to pay up."

"Oh! let me go!" and with a sudden movement she got her arm away, and ran round the corner.

"Ha! ha! ha! ha! didn't I frighten that gal? Am I so jolly ugly lookin'? Say, old Fagan, come here. I've lost you a customer, I have. Ha! ha! ha!" The old man came to the door, very angry.

"Vat for you do that? and vat for you call me old Fagan?"

"Because you look like an old fellow of that name I've heard of."

"Vat for you drive my customers away, hey?"

"She's got a stunnin' trinket—a picture with real pearls and diamants round it. I was in a hurry to see how you'd cheat her, so I offered her an introduce, but your ugly phiz frightened her away. Ha! ha! ha!"

"Vat for you lie so? She no see me; vat for you stay about my shop frightening nice ladies away? You go, or I call a police."

"You old lummicks! Is that all the thanks I get for trying to bring you a customer? The next shirt or coat you get from me for a three penny bit, you can put in your eye, and still see to cheat as well as ever."

"You—you—you go, now, or I get cross—very much angry!"

"Who cares for your anger, old skinflint? You ought to brag of your shop, for everything goes in, and precious little comes out."

"You mean to say I no give fair price? You go way now!" and he became very angry.

"You know you are an old cheat; that's what makes you so riley!"

"Police! police!"

"If that's your game, old Surly, I won't trouble you any more with my company. Good-night, old Hunks!" and whistling, he sauntered away.

"That is a bad young man; he will dance on a cord some day, if he no be careful; it won't be under his feet, eder, but just under his left ear!" and chuckling he entered his shop.

After some time, Clare returned, and looking about, thought:

" Is he gone ? I do not see him; why did he annoy me so ? Should he come again what could I do ? But I must be courageous, or have no where to stay to-night."

The old man came to the door of his shop, and seeing her, said in a wheedling voice:

"Come in my little teer! Vat have you got purty to show me? Come in; I always pays goot prices?"

"It is my mother's portrait—I—I do not wish to sell it only to leave it as security for what money you will let me have."

"Oh! it's a purty lady! Vat is des around it ? Little bits of glass?"

"No, sir; they are diamonds and pearls."

"Imitation, you mean!" and he looked over his spectacles scrutin- izingly.

"No, sir, real; it's a gift from my dear mother; please say what money you can loan me."

"Vell, not much, not much."

"But how much ?"

"Vell," and he rubbed his chin contemplatively, "three shillings!"

"Oh! sir, that would scarcely pay a night's lodging."

" Vell, money ish scarce ; worth ten per cent. a month ; very scarce. Vell, I vill be very goot, for you are a nice lady ; I give you five shillings."

" Is that all ? Then I must go somewhere else ; and as she still had hold of the long chain, she tried to draw the locket from his his hand.

" Eh ?   Perhaps you stole him!" and he jerked the chain from her grasp, and called quickly, but not in a very loud voice, "police! police!"

" Oh! don't—don't call the police ; I will take anything."

" I ought to call the police, but I am a goot man—got tender heart —here's five shillings."

" Thank you ; I will come for it again and give you guineas for your trouble !" and Clare almost ran back to the inn, while the old man, rubbing his hands and chuckling, re-entered his shop on the alert for another victim.

Chapter XVII.

Willet and Cubby's little romance had come to a climax, that is a dramatic climax ; they had got married.   They were enacting a little domestic scene in the grand hall that led to the drawing room in the Dudley mansion.   There was a magnificent ball and party going on in honor of the Lady Elmer's safe return.

Willet was one of those coquettish wives who like to display their power over their husbands, so she accidentally, apparently, dropped her handkerchief, and called, " Cubby!"

" Yes, dear," and he came to her side with a series of quick little steps, that showed a slight fear, mingled with his love.

"My handkerchief."

" Yes, love ; and with the same quick step he brought it to her.

" Thank you.   How long have we been married, dear ?"

" Seven days!" and he unconsciously sighed.

" Cubby!" reproachfully, " why do you sigh?"

" From—from excess of joy, love!" he answered quickly.

"Ah! then please give your joy a more pleasant expression."

"Yes, love. Ha! ha! ha!"

"Cubby! This is an occasion on which you can show yourself the loving, obedient husband. This is an occasion on which to make me envied even by my betters; for who possesses a loving obedient husband without being proud of him. And you're a good-looking man, too!" she took his arm, and walked a few steps, he looked silily pleased, "and appear better smiling than sighing," and she patted his cheek. "I've a secret to tell you; I have perceived your fine business qualities, so am going to let you invest to the best advantage, some little savings of mine."

"I didn't know I married an heiress!" said Cubby, quite proud.

"And now, dear Cubby, I want you to do me a favor—use all your influence, which is great, I know, to bring about a match between my lady and your master; then, dear, we shall not be separated again, and with both our perquisites, in a few years we can start in business for ourselves and be independent."

"Then you're not a woman's rights man?"

She laughed merrily. "Did you think so because I wanted an obedient husband? Oh! we ladies all like that, yet you shall always be the business man; but the house, you know, must be my kingdom."

"Give us a kiss to bind the bargain!" and he gave her an old-fashioned kiss or rather hug, putting his arms around her neck and squeezing her.

"Cubby, fix my ruff."

"Yes, love."

"Thank you!" and they went to their respective duties, proud and happy.

Chapter XVIII.

From the street, the house illuminated in every window, the garden
hung with Chinese lanterns, the elegantly dressed ladies and gentlemen
visible in the drawing room, made a very pretty picture; so thought
the bad young man Dick, who had so frightened poor Clare.   He had
quietly stolen in the back way, to get a nearer view.

"My heyes! ain't this a stunnin' show?" thought he, as he peeped
into the long French window that opened on to the balcony, but a
few feet from the rising lawn.   "Shouldn't I like to have one of them
angels in silk for a pard in a few steps of the mazurk," and as the
music sounded tantalizing and inspiring, he took his coat tails in his
hands and had a little dance on the green all by himself.   When the
music and dancing ceased, the servants handed around ices and sherbet, and Dick smacked his lips, saying, "Hi! but I'd like to be in
there!" then as Lady Downington came on the balcony, he thought,
"some one coming.   I must make myself scarce!" and he did so, as
Lady Downington called :

"Jonquil! Jonquil! Where can he be?   The night air will injure
this poor darling.   Jonquil! I say!"   And Jonquil, coming from the
side of the house where several of the servants had been watching the
dancers and gossipping, reported :

"Here, my lady."

"Where have you been?   I've been calling and calling you. Master 'Pinkette' will be quite ill breathing this night air on an empty
stomach; take him to the pantry and give him of the best you can
procure."

"Yes, my lady." And she leaned over the balcony railings and placed the dog tenderly in his arms, saying: "Now be very careful."

"Yes, my lady;" and he disappeared from her view, as she entered the ball room again, saying :

"That man is invaluable."

Each night Clare had stolen from the little inn, and watched the Dudley mansion. She had seen Sir Francis enter several times, and her heart was nearly broken. She had heard nothing from her mother, and had been compelled to pawn part of her underclothes to enable her to live this long. This very night she had determined, after her watching was over, to seek her home at all hazards, and see what was the matter.

She entered the garden as the musicians came from the house, and some of the ladies and gentlemen followed, and danced on the smooth cut grass; Elmer led the quadrille; then the music changed into a polka, and they danced into the house again, the servants enjoying the sight vastly. And Clare watched.

"How happy they are all here, while I am in such misery. He is not here at least. Oh! I am so thankful he cherishes my memory, and she with all her beauty and vast wealth cannot fascinate him from me. Life is still endurable. Who of my old time friends are here?" and she went to the window and looked into the room.

Sir Francis came from the house, to indulge in thought for a moment in quietness.

"Can I be mistaken? Is Lady Elmer innocent? I've watched her so closely since the night of the pretended robbery, yet cannot tell by word or look, what is in her heart. Always speaking of her friend Clare, and urging me still to try some new plan to effect her release. When I mention the poor girls in the boat, she seems to feel so sorry for their fate, and wonders who they were, when I know her glass is more powerful than mine, and their features must have been quite visible to her. Was the resemblance to Clare only a delusion of my brain? If it were only so, I should have a better and a nobler object in life than trying to discover a woman's treachery."

Elmer missed him immediately and soon sent Willet with a message. She readily found him, and courtesying, said:

"My lord, my lady says they are about to play a beautiful sonatus of Mosesheart that you would be sorry to miss."

With all his grief he could not help smiling.

"A sonata of Mozart's you mean."

"I expect so, sir;" and she dropped a courtesy. "I knew it was something with a heart in it; and it is a pity, sir, that some gentlemen don't have more heart for them that care so much for them." And she walked quickly into the house.

"What can the girl mean? Now for another trial. Will it never cease?" And Clare saw him just as he was entering the door.

"That was Sir Francis. What does he here in this gay scene, thinking me still in prison? Has—has he ceased to love me?" Then she looked into the window again. "How her face brightens as he enters the room. Ah! they are coming to this window!" and she crouched down beneath the balcony. As the music began they came out, and Elmer said:

"Francis—Sir Francis, will you not sit here and enjoy this exquisite music of Mozart?"

"Ah! that indeed falls soothingly on my unhappy heart."

"Have we not done everything in our power? Then why indulge in such constant melancholy? It is not kind to your friends who love you so."

"I am not satisfied. I shall take the next ship that sails to Australia and ascertain for a certainty if the lady is safe. Should she not have perished in the ocean, for I fear that face in the boat was no delusion, I will remain near her till freedom or death releases her from her terrible captivity."

"Oh! do not go, Sir Francis. I—I—too, have suffered so much! Would you not pity a woman who loved so intensely that she had periled her soul for that love? I—I—"

Clare starting up, shrieked:

"Oh! I am betrayed!" and fell insensible to the earth.

Chapter XIX.

Elmer hearing a woman had fainted in the garden ordered her to be taken into a pleasant, quiet room up stairs away from the sound of the music and voices. She was naturally a kind hearted, generous woman, and had she not been transformed by her ill-fated love, the world would have been the better for her living in it.

Clare had sunk into a sleep of deep exhaustion, and seeing her comfortable, the servant had left her. But now it was morning and the sun high up; still Clare slept on; it was the first time for so many months that she had lain in a bed like those in her own home. When she awoke it was nearly noon, and for awhile her senses were confused. " Have I been ill, or dreaming ?" She thought. Then she raised herself on her elbow. " Was I the inmate of a prison escaping with great peril ? That night on the ocean; was it real or only delusion ? Oh! the dreadful shame of that trial! But I am awake now, and in a beautiful room. This is not my mother's house! It all comes back to me now!" She was standing on the floor in an instant. "I am in the house of the one woman of all the world who is my enemy. I will hide no more, leaving her free, like a serpent to twine around his heart and steal his love from me. I will denounce her for the wretch she is! Oh! that I could meet her face to face."

Elmer, drawn by an irresistible impulse, entered the room.

" My maid tells me you rested well last night. I trust you only fainted from fatigue. Had you walked far ?"

Clare turned and faced her, saying in a quiet, intense voice :

"Do you not know me, Elmer Dudley?"

But she shrieked in terror :

"It is her ghost!"

"Ah! your conscience speaks at last. But I am not dead yet."

"Is it really my Clare escaped in safety?" and she went quickly toward her. But Clare stepped back, saying :

"Come not near; your touch would poison me."

"Oh! my dear friend, your trouble has unnerved you."

"Your friend! And how have you deserved that title from me?"

"Did I not prove my friendship by going all those weary miles to aid in your release ?" But Clare laughed bitterly.

"Oh! how well you performed your mission of mercy! You betrayed me to the Governor and set a price upon my head."

"Oh, my poor Clare! Is then your reason clouded at last ?"

"Oh, no; I am quite sane. Even that night on the terrible ocean, nearly perishing with thirst, not knowing what moment we might be pursued, and I taken back to a captivity worse than death, even that night did not obscure my mind or make me for one moment forget my heartless wrongs."

"Oh, my friend, who could have wronged you to change your gentle nature thus ?"

"Do you ask me ? Oh, arch hypocrite, what had I done, how darkened your life, that you should pursue me like an unrelenting fiend ?"

"Have a care! "

"Too late; you have done your worst!"

"Ah!"

"On that night, under the flimsy pretext that you were robbed, you cast a shade upon that honor which for five hundred years had shone so brightly. Elmer Dudley, what had I done ?"

"What had you done? I will tell you. With your soft voice and your yellow hair you had stolen away that heart I would have periled my soul to gain."

"Ah! you confess it. With soft words you drew my secret from me, then you turned traitor to long years of friendship; you forgot every attribute of a womanly heart to banish and disgrace me, so that Sir Francis, in the bitterness of his grief, would accept your consolation. But that will be never."

"Ah! you are mistaken; for is he not nightly by my side, hanging on my every word, envious of the very night that separates us ?"

"False, false, as your guilt-stained heart!"

"Then I will make it true! I will give you back into the clutches of the law—"

"Ah!"

"Should you again escape, I will hunt you from every place of refuge, and follow you to the death!"

"Perjured woman, though you should make me suffer a thousand deaths, you can never gain his love; for in his heart he hates, nay, despises you !"

"You shall never witness it."

"You placed the diamonds in my handkerchief. You bribed the captain to leave us to perish on the ocean! But we were saved, and I am here to denounce you to his face; he shall see what a monster would claim his love!"

"Help! help!"

"Perjurer!"

"Help! help, to secure this mad woman."

"Murderess!"

"Help! help!" and Lady Elmer rushed from the room shrieking and calling for help, till the whole house was aroused.

Clare stood like one in a dream, but the hurrying footsteps awoke her.

"Ah! she will have me secured and taken to a mad house! then I should never see him, and he would be in the power of that fiend who has neither conscience nor mercy; that shall never be!" Then without pausing, as the footsteps came nearer, she sprung from the window, and falling on the soft earth of a flower-bed, was only slightly bruised and breathless; in a moment she was on her feet, and fleeing like a deer.

But Elmer, whose carriage was waiting for her, hastily ordered the coachman to drive to the nearest police station, and her foot was on the steps, when Clare, dashing from the window, frightened the horses, who, starting madly, threw the coachman from his seat, and dragged her to the gate, where striking her head against a post, the horses flew down the road, leaving her bleeding, crushed and senseless.

Chapter XX.

In the horror that follows a dreadful accident, people seem stunned and incapable of affording that help their ordinary good sense would enable them to. So it was in the case of Lady Elmer; her father was absent, and the servants let her lay where she was thrown for some little time; one of them even suggested, with the superstition of ignorance, that they had better not move her till the "crowner" came. But Willet's wits came to her soonest, and she had her carried into the nearest room, then ran for Cubby.

"Cubby! oh, dear! oh, dear! what a dreadful accident. Cubby!

Cubby! quick, quick!" But he not having heard of the accident came to her quite leisurely.

"What's all this noise about, Mrs. Cubby?"

"Quick, you lazy man, quick, and go for the doctor."

"What! are you so very ill?"

"Stupid! don't you know her ladyship is nearly killed? That Lady Clare jumping from the window frightened the horses just as her ladyship was on the carriage step, and I don't know how many limbs is broken?"

"Oh! the poor lady! We handsome sex have much to answer for."

"Yes—for making a—well a dunce of some of us. But are you going to let her ladyship die, while you stop here to praise yourself?"

"Well, no; as it isn't you, I should have no object."

"Oh! you cruel wretch!" and she burst out crying. "I'll—I'll get a divorce."

"You can't my dear. I never treated you with extreme cruelty."

"What! not cruel to wish me dead?"

"Why, my dear, how you misunderstand a man. I said it wasn't you that was nearly killed; I said—"

"There don't stop here to tell me what you said, or I'll go myself."

"But—"

"Go along, I say, or it may be too late."

"But—"

"None of your 'buts' but go!" and she put his hat upon his head and pushed him out of the door. "Well, some men are as stubborn as mules, and have as large ears, too!" She would liked to have made Cubby's a little larger, too, by pulling, but suddenly recollecting that she had left her lady insensible, she hurried back to her, forgetting all her own petty little annoyances.

•

Chapter XXI.

Lady Clare concealed herself till night came, them fled to her own home. But no loving mother awaited her. The house was closed, dark and deserted. What should she do ? She must find shelter for the night without exposing herself to be again arrested. So she stole around to the back of the garden and tried the little gate. What was her joy to find it open. She went in quickly but very quietly, up the path she knew so well and under the beautiful trees. When near the house, a light like a star of hope shone from one of the servants' win‑ dows. She rapped gently at the door, but no one opened it; she rapped again a little louder; still she could hear no movement inside and her heart sank within her. Yet she would not give up, but knocked once more, still louder, and listened. Soon she heard the sound of a pair of pattens; she knew the sound and her heart sent up a prayer of thanks; it was her old nurse, Ruth. But the moment the door was opened, and the light of the woman's candle fell upon her face she uttered a shriek.

"Oh, poor Lady Clare, is it your ghost come back ?"

" 'Sh! No, Ruth, let me in, quick. I am hungry, hunted, and so faint with fatigue "

"Oh, my poor child!" and old Ruth closed and barred the door; then putting her arm around her, led her to her own cosy bedroom, where, although it was summer, a fire was burning. "Now don't speak, dear, till I give you a cup of tea, and you have eaten and warmed yourself, for deary, deary, how cold you are!" and the old lady quickly spread the cloth, and taking the tea from the hob, where it stayed from morning till night always ready; then cutting some bread, she quickly toasted it, and buttered it generously; then placing cold meat and jam upon the table, she pushed it close to Clare and bade her eat. She was so hungry, having scarcely eaten anything since she left the ship, that she obeyed the old woman like a docile child. She was so faint and weak that she could not even ask about her mother. She took the cup eagerly, but her poor hand trembled so that she nearly let it fall.

"Ah! poor dear! you shall first drink a little of my home made wine." She drank a glass, then ate eagerly of the food. It seemed to her a banquet for the gods! Her chilled blood was warmed and her numbed senses aroused.

"Ruth—"

"Nay! don't talk till ye have drank the tea." So she ate a little more, and drank the tea; then she felt stronger.

"My mother, Ruth, where is she? Not dead, or my heart would have told me."

"No, my lady, she has gone to India, to consult your brother what to do for you." Then Clare told her how she had made her escape, and the terrible night on the ocean—everything except the scene with Elmer Dudley.

"Now, Ruth, is there so secret room in this old mansion, where I could go in case of danger?"

" No really secret room, but there is a room that no one but the family and servant's know of; it has no windows, only a small skylight; the door is very low and concealed behind that stately old oak chair in the library."

" Oh ! yes; I remember hearing that it led to an old lumber room up stairs. But, dear Ruth, I shall not leave you till danger threatens. Now I will write to my mother, telling her everything, and beg her to hasten home ; then I will go to bed, for I am very tired." So she wrote a long, loving letter. Then Ruth arranged a nice soft bed for her in her room, and told her not to fear, for she would be near her all night long, and was a light sleeper; the least noise would arouse her. Then she stroked her hair, till she fell into a gentle slumber, and falling on her knees she thanked Heaven for her darling's escape, then kissing her gently, she, too, went to rest.

Chapter XXII.

At Lady Dudley's five of the finest physicians and surgeons of London were holding a consultation over the injuries of Lady Elmer. They decided that it would not be necessary—at least they did not think so at present—to amputate any of her limbs, though she was dreadfully bruised and had several bones broken.

Lady Elmer, with hearing sharpened by intense suffering and eagerness to know her fate, heard nearly all the whispered consultation, and the possibility implied that she yet might lose a limb, made her hatred of Lady Clare so increase in strength and bitterness that she hardly felt the terrible pain. The family doctor asked her if she would take chloroform while the terrible gash in her forehead was being sewed; she replied no; she could endure it. But when he saw that the pain caused her to press her teeth so deeply into her lip that the blood welled up, he would have pressed the chloroformed handkerchief over mouth and nose even against her will; but the scintillating fire of her eyes was fixed on him so steadily that he dared not. At each fresh pain she vowed in her heart to have a terrible revenge upon the one who caused her loss of soul, and almost body, too. Then they set her broken leg, but not a groan escaped her; her pain seemed to give her a fiendish joy, that now she had justification for any cruelty toward Lady Clare. The room was darkened, and she all bandaged and bound up, was left with an opiate, and some one to watch but not talk. But what opiate would set at rest a brain like hers, whose heart was every second sending thither streams of wicked blood, keeping it even more active for evil than it had been for months before ?

Thus she lay for weeks and weeks ; though crippled and helpless, her will still ruled the whole household. She told her father, who was a mild, loving man, completely under her sway, that she wished two detectives to be kept constantly watching the De Mille Mansion, and if Lady Clare was seen to leave or enter, or any indications of her presence there were discovered, she should be immediately informed.

Willet had become very sympathetic for the proud, beautiful lady who suffered so intensely for love, for though no one knew what had occurred between the two ladies, yet Clare was recognized and held responsible for Elmer's dreadful accident. So all the servants became private detectives, and whenever they had an afternoon out, were sure to pass the De Mille Mansion to see what they could discover; and one venturesome and romantic young chambermaid, even went so far as to ring the front door bell on some pretended errand, but no one appeared, although she waited for a whole quarter of an hour.

Sir Francis had heard all the servants' gossip from Cubby, who lived a part of his time with his wife at Lord Dudley's. He pitied Lady Elmer, for he was now forced to believe that all her wickedness was caused by her love for him; so he sent his card twice a week with wishes for her recovery. Each time she received it, she gnashed her teeth and muttered:

"He does not love me, or he would come." Then a spasm of pain would seem almost to stop the beating of her heart; there she would lay, deathly pale and quivering, till Willet, becoming frightened, would wet her face with cologne, and try to arouse her.

She was indeed to be pitied, for a woman who could love so intensely, that terrible bodily pain became almost pleasure, endured for his dear sake, that guilt, nay, even crime, were looked upon as only means to the yearned-for end—where death itself, would have been accepted with more than a martyr's enthusiasm, to gain from him one smile of returning love—was entitled to be viewed through the vail of sweet charity.

At length her wounds were healed, and she was allowed to sit up some hours each day; but the beautiful peace that the convalescent feels; the dreamy pleasure only to view the changing clouds; the luxury of sitting by the open window and breathing the fresh air; the resurrection, as it were, seeing the world which had been dead for many weeks alive again; the indescribable joy of life and returning health, were as dross to her. All these sweet feelings were merged into love dangerously fierce, and a purpose of swift and dire revenge.

As the days went by, and she found that she was a cripple, and would most likely remain one through life, one leg being shorter than the other, and her side and arm partially paralyzed, drawing one eye down slightly, her rage knew no bounds. The servants fled from her presence, and even Willet, who had made of her a heroine of romance, gladly hid herself in some closet. The scar on her forehead was red and fierce, and when for the first time since the accident, she looked into the glass, she gave a scream of horror, and with the stick she used for a support, she shattered it to pieces. Her father coming in, she told him to have the cruel things removed from every parlor and room in the house, or she would serve them likewise.

Never once in all her long weeks of pain, had a thought entered her mind against herself. The feelings of love and revenge had, like a simoom, burnt up every tender feeling of a woman's heart, and left her a wreck to make angels weep. One day she said:

"That woman is at her home, I feel it; and shall she enjoy life and love, while I, who have lost so much, am living in a mental hell? Willet, bring me word to-night, or never enter this house again."

Willet dared not answer, but tremblingly put on a slight disguise, and went to do her bidding. She passed and repassed the De Mille

Mansion, but could see no face at any of the windows; the front steps were covered with dust, and grass growing in the pathways. She went to the back gate, and her heart jumped to find it open. She went in stealthily; she felt like a thief—looked everywhere, but could see or hear nothing; becoming bolder, she tried the door, but it was locked; she must get some news for her lady, but how? After thinking and thinking, she determined to go to the grocer's where they dealt; for if the Lady Clare was at home she must eat, and as two would eat more than one—the detective had reported that the house was in charge of an old woman, she could find out if more than usual were ordered, but she would have to go to work very delicately; so selecting a clerk that looked good-natured and communicative, she asked for a couple of pounds of sugar, some coffee, and had it ground, and a few other things that took time to put up, all the while chatting with the young man.

"The poor Lady Clare's at home again!" So she tried to find out what he knew. ''Have you heard how she is?"

''Well, now, you don't say so! The old lady that has been minding the house is a great object of interest to us all, and we noticed that lately she orders more delicacies—in fact, more of everything. So, so, the poor lady's back again. Well, well, I'm glad of it."

Willet had learned all she wanted, so hastened home and reported to Lady Elmer, whose face lit up with triumph.

''Ah! now I can have my revenge! Can the mother have returned too?"

"I think not, my lady."

"Then I shall have to wait. Oh! the days seem years, the time passes so slowly. Oh! how old I am! Give me my writing materials."

In a few moments Willet had a letter directed to Lady Clare De Mille, and was on her way to post it.

Chapter XXIII.

For many weeks Lady Clare lived in perfect seclusion. When the street bell rang she hastened to the secret room, and there amid old furniture, worm eaten and dusty, the silken hangings dropping away piecemeal, old pictures of remote ancestors long since dead and forgotten, whose eyes stared at her in the semi-darkness, trunks of old letters and boxes of musty books, she would sit for hours. The idea of being again arrested, was her haunting terror. The cobwebs and dust of years covered the little skylight window; it was a weird, ghostly place. To keep herself from becoming nervous in the long hours of waiting and suspense, she would read the old letters. The correspondence of each writer was tied in a separate parcel, with little bits of dingy, faded ribbon.

What a world of new experience the old trunk opened to her! For awhile she would forget her own trouble, sympathizing with that of another. One packet of letters began when the writer was a young girl—clear, delicate, aristocratic writing—then came her marriage, then trouble, then little children cheered her. The letters were sometimes years apart, but the trouble seemed always there; then the writing grew tremulous, and then ceased. Clare gave a sigh of relief, thinking how pleasant it must be for kindly death to relieve one from terrible misery or trouble.

One thing cheered her—that was the daily receipt of a loving letter from Sir Francis. She always answered it, but begged he would not come to see her, and thus expose her to the realization of her terrible dread.

He had sent Lady De Mille several telegrams; finally one intercepted her on her journey, and she hastened back with all speed.

The day before Lady De Mille arrived, Clare was all excitement; she had just received Elmer's letter. It said:

"LADY CLARE DE MILLE: The third of June will be the anniversary of that day on which I learned that which has wrecked my life. I beg you will have all your friends assembled, and as many of mine as witnessed the occurrences of that night, as possible. I wish to do an act, without the performance of which I could not die happy. Your mother will have returned by then, and can make every preparation.
"ELMER DUDLEY."

"Ah! she wishes to declare my innocence! Her sufferings have softened her heart." She had read of her terrible injuries and daily reports of her health, in the papers Ruth always brought her. "And now she will render me tardy justice, but how can she obliterate the memory of the pain and anguish, the shame, she has caused me? But it is past now, and I will only think of the future—the happy future! Poor Elmer! she, too, has suffered. If I could, I would make her well again, and as beautiful as ever. What does she say? my mother will be here? Oh! that cannot be possible! So soon! No, it is too much joy for one day." Then she called Ruth, and told her the good news. She was so excited, that she laughed and cried at the same moment; then throwing herself in Ruth's arms, she sobbed as though her heart would break.

"Don'tee, dear, don'tee ; your troubles will soon be over. Oh ! don'tee, or—or I shall cry, too !" and with the word the tears came, and so they relieved their over-burdened hearts.

"There, that will do," said Clare, wiping her eyes. "'Now I feel like another Clare ; not the sad, despondent one of an hour ago, but the light-hearted, happy Clare of other days." Old Ruth smiled, too, then Clare ran away, and for the first time since her return, she wandered all over the house, into every room. The furniture and ornaments seemed like old friends, and she greeted them as such. In her mother's room she sat in the great easy chair and laid her cheek against it."

" Dear mother, how often has your loved head rested here," and she kissed the insensate covering, "and soon it will again." And her heart sent up a prayer of thanks for this foretaste of happiness. She even ventured to take a hasty glance out of the window, which heretofore she had avoided, as though certain death would have been the penalty for the indulgence of her curiosity. But now the terrible dread seemed to lessen as the time of the vindication of her innocence drew near, for who could wish her re-arrest, when Elmer herself had repented the wrong she had done her ? How beautiful the garden looked! The weeks of neglect had only enhanced its wild luxuriance. The mignonette, gilly flower, and heliotrope filled the air with the most delicious and grateful of perfumes. Gorgeous butterflies seemed to have come from all parts of the island, to make this quiet, undisturbed spot their home. The birds sang on the trees in a fearless way she had never known before. When her mother returned, it would be indeed home to her, more valued and appreciated than ever.

Old Ruth now ventured to pick a nosegay for her dear child; and never were flowers that did not come from a lover so caressed and talked to. Had she known the day on which her mother was to return, she would have had each room bright with these sweet children of the sunshine, for some hearts love them with such peculiar tenderness, that it is almost pain to pluck them from their parent stems, and as for wantonly hurting or destroying them, they would as soon think of hurting a little child.

This night she slept so peacefully, without those fearful starts waking her, bathed in perspiration and seeing handcuffs, prisons and chains, till sleep had become almost a torture. In the morning she wrote to Sir Francis; telling him how happy she was, and all that Elmer was going to do; for in her heart she did not doubt but that she was about to make her all the reparation in her power for what she had caused her to suffer. Then laying a slip of scented lemon and one of heliotrope within the letter, she kissed it and soon it was in the hands of her delighted lover. But he almost doubted the reality of Elmer's sudden repentance, yet it was not impossible, as intense pain has often been known to soften the heart.

Later in the day, when a carriage rolled up to the door and Lady De Mille alighted, Clare could scarely restrain herself from rushing down the stairs, out to the gate and into her mother's arms.

What a meeting was theirs! Not to be described, only to be felt.

The servants all came flocking back, as if summoned by magic, and there was sweeping and scrubbing and dusting; and boxes and baskets and hampers arrived each hour. All seemed joyous bustle and confusion. Dainty notes were sent all over the city, and gossip said the De Milles were going to give a magnificent party, and gossip wondered if the Lady Clare had been pardoned, and if she hadn't been it was a burning shame that her mother could be so gay and her daughter in prison. And if she had been, they would like to know why poor women were left to serve out their long terms, and the rich let off thus easily.

Still the preparations went on, yet no one saw the Lady Clare and friends and enemies alike wondered what was to be the end.

For several days she had not heard from Sir Francis, and only that she had perfect faith in him her heart would have been troubled.

"It is all for the best," she would say to herself gently. "He is thinking of me and perhaps even now doing something for my good." Her mother encouraged her in this belief, so that since the arrival of Elmer's letter, she had not had an unhappy moment.

And it was the eve of the grand party.

Chapter XXIV.

The carriages were arriving rapidly. The beautiful De Mille
Mansion was transformed from the deserted, neglected pile of the last
few months, into a fairy palace of light, flowers, perfume and music.
In the ladies' dressing-room was a bevy of beautiful women, indulging
in the fashionable pastime, gossip.

Gossip is a much maligned, scandalized goddess. She has her uses
but not her abuses; for when gossip ceases, there is silence; what the
world considers her abuses is something very different altogether—
scandal or twaddle.

Gossip is intellectual food, brightening our daily life, raising our
thoughts above the little corroding annoyances, strengthening us,
polishing off the rust accumulated by constant communion with undeveloped intellects. Gossip is the kindly interest in our neighbor's
affairs, that would not prompt a word to harm, that only likes to
praise and please; the interchange of ideas developed by different
circumstances, the gathering of information—useful information that
no books can teach us.

Beautiful goddess! Men love thee, even better than thy humble
sisters, women; they spend, too, more time in thy worship, smoking
fragrant incense at thy shrine, but coward-like, they call thee Business
and Tobacco!

One gentle girl, the Lady Annie, said to a beauty by her side :

'' Oh, I am so glad the Lady Clare is back again. She is so sweet
and lovely.''

'' Have you seen her ?'' asked the other eagerly.

'' No; but she must have returned, or why this party ?''

"Has she been seen by any one you know ?" She replied in the
negative. "How strange! neither have I heard of any one who has

seen her." Thus they talked on for some time, coming to no conclusion but that it was very strange, and they were curious to know
how it would end.

"But I saw Lady Elmer; you remember how beautiful she was ?"
A nod in reply. "Well, she is not even passable now. I've heard hints
of what frightened the horses, but nothing definite enough to satisfy
curiosity, so I am here to-night ready for any romantic adventure to
occur!" and the beauty drew on her long kid glove.

In the garden Lady Downington and her dog, attended by her
faithful courtier, Butterfly, paused a few moments before entering the
house.

"Well, Butterfly, this is the most tantalizing affair I was ever engaged in. Of course, I don't ask you to love Lady Elmer any longer,
knowing how fond you are of beauty."

"No, no; I—I should be afraid of her! She looks so fierce in
her carriage." This was the longest sentence his lordship had been
ever known to say, and this was brought out by fright, thinking Lady
Downington might insist on his marrying Elmer, whether or no.

"Ahem! Butterfly, what do you think of Lady Clare ?"

"Oh! ah! that would be so—so romantic!" But Lady Downington
did not know if her match-making powers were equal to this, so she
said no more on that subject.

"Well, Butterfly, Lady Elmer will be here to-night and perhaps she
will not look as bad as we think; it was in a dim light that I saw her.
She urged me to come to-night, why, I cannot tell; it can't be to meet
Lady Clare, for I've heard nothing of her pardon. Well, we shall
soon unravel the mystery. Let us go in;" and Lady Downington
joined the other ladies in the dressing room. From the moment of
her entrance, there was no lack of twaddle with an occasional sprinkling of something crueller.

Clare was in her room, pale as the costly dress she wore. "What does it mean?" she thought. "No word from Sir Francis and in a few moments I must be in the ball room. Elmer, too, has she at last succeeded and stolen him from me? No, I will not have an unkind thought against him!" Her mother came in, and kissing her, said:

"Dear child, do not look so sad. Remember this is the last night of your dreadful trouble; then Sir Francis shall wait no longer for his bride."

"That is it; why have we not heard from him? Why is he not here? Oh! mother, if he is false, this night would indeed end all my troubles!" But the mother kissed and petted her, saying:

" Bear up only a few hours more, darling, then if our hopes are not realized, it will be time enough for despair. But you really ought to rejoice, for Sir Francis is without doubt engaged in one more effort for our benefit. Will you not come into the drawing-room?"

" Not yet, dear mother; how could I bear the congratulations of our friends, for what? Not till Sir Francis or Elmer Dudley comes to declare my innocence, will I expose myself to such humiliation. Go you and receive our guests; but the moment they arrive send me word, and I will come down."

So Lady De Mille went to the drawing-room, and received her guests with smiling graciousness, though her heart bled for poor Clare up stairs. The company were too well bred to even hint she had a daughter, but they wondered, and wondered, and wondered, and the time flew by.

Not wishing to have any of these awkward pauses that give so much latitude for surmise, Lady De Mille led the dance herself.

"Lady Downington, please tell me why we are here to-night?" asked the Lady Annie.

"Well, child, you are asking more than I can tell. I supposed it was to congratulate the Lady Clare on her release, but I see I was mistaken, as she has not even been mentioned, let alone seen."

"Oh! I am so disappointed. But why did her mother give this party then? Do you suppose she expected her also, and is more bitterly disappointed than any of us?"

"It is not too late for something to happen yet. I cannot think all these costly and elegant preparations were made only to give the old lady a chance to dance. But I like to dance myself, so excuse me till I put this little darling into safe hands, then I shall join the next quadrille." Then Lady Annie sought the beauty. She was beginning to feel so sorry for the poor mother, who could not hide how eagerly she watched the door, and whose face, when the smile for a moment departed, looked as if drawn by pain.

"Is it not too bad?" she said. "What can have happened?"

"Oh, there will be a denouement yet!" the beauty replied.

But when the hours flew by, and supper was announced, the surprise and wonder knew no bounds; yet Lady De Mille smiled and sat at the head of her table.

Up stairs Clare counted the moments by heart-throbs. "Will they never come? Oh! I shall die, I shall die!"

Her nerves were strung to such a high tension, that it seemed the least shock would break them, and leave her a quivering thing of beauty without a mind.

She heard the rustling garments, as the ladies came from supper; she heard the servants' gossip on the stairs; she heard the exquisite music, as the dancers danced; she heard that same lovely sonata of Mozart's. She could have shrieked in agony. As the last strains died away, the servant announced in the distance, but to Clare it seemed shouted in her ears in stentorian tones—

"Lady Elmer Dudley!"

She sprang to her feet, shook out her dress, gave a hasty glance in the mirror—she was Eve's daughter—and in a moment she stood within the drawing room door, where Elmer was bowing to the company.

Oh! what a wreck she looked! Where was all her proud beauty? Where the fascinating glance? Where the queenly dignity? Alas! even Clare pitied her, and a murmur of sympathy for her dreadful misfortune filled the room.

"My friends, this is my birthday. You all know what happened one year ago to-night. You all know how I tried to save my friend —went to Australia, offered my fortune, periled my life! You see me now this dreadful wreck—this poor, pitiful satire of a woman— this maimed and crippled mass, rendered so by the fiend it tried to save! You see her there, smiling in her beauty, her lace and pearls hiding her false heart. You see her there, *the escaped convict, Clare De Mille!*"

But she did not faint; conscious of her innocence, she stood there facing her enemy, and dauntlessly looked her in the eye.

"Oh! I could not die in peace till I had sent her back to where she belonged, among thieves and murderers! Officers, arrest that woman! She is a tried and condemned thief, trying to escape her just punishment!"

Two policemen appeared as if summoned by the evil one, and laid their hands upon Clare's shoulder.

"Elmer Dudley, God will avenge me!"

They seized her uplifted hand, and pressing the rude iron on her delicate wrist, it closed with a sound that sent a shudder through the room, and aroused the mother, who seemed to have been turned to stone.

"No, no, no! you shall not take her again! My inocent child! it will kill her! Take me instead! Where—where is Sir Francis? He will not let you go! He will die, if need be, to save you!"

The ladies were sobbing now, and all was excitement and pity.

The other handcuff closed with a click, and all hope died out of poor Clare's heart.

"Oh, my mother! I cannot go!"

"Nor shall you, darling!" Sir Francis stood in the door.

"Ah! that loved voice! I am saved!"

"Officers, do you recognize this seal? This is from her Majesty, the Queen of England, declaring the innocence of Lady Clare De Mille!"

In a moment they were in each other's arms, and where the policeman had stood, appeared a white robed minister. After a moment's consultation, Clare and Sir Francis stood before him. The sound of a sword clanged on the marble steps, and the brother from India was in time to give his sister to the man she loved.

As their hands were joined, Elmer, with a hiss like a wounded serpent, rushed from the house, and from that hour, she was never seen again outside her own home, by friend or foe.

But a life of happiness rewarded the Lady Clare for all her sufferings.